Howard Pay

The Boy Scouts At the Canadian Border

Howard Payson

The Boy Scouts At the Canadian Border

1st Edition | ISBN: 978-3-75234-689-3

Place of Publication: Frankfurt am Main, Germany

Year of Publication: 2020

Outlook Verlag GmbH, Germany.

Reproduction of the original.

THE BOY SCOUTS
AT THE CANADIAN BORDER

By LIEUT. HOWARD PAYSON

CHAPTER I
A GLIMPSE OVER INTO CANADA

"Suppose we hold up here, and rest a bit, fellows!"

"We'll have to accommodate you, Tubby. It really pains me to hear you puffing and blowing so hard."

"Now, that's just six words for me and half a dozen for yourself, Andy Bowles. Haven't I seen you look longingly at every log we passed, as if you wished Rob would give the order to sit down and recuperate? Honest to goodness, I do own up that I'm a trifle winded. This pack seems to keep on getting heavier and heavier."

"You only imagine it does, Tubby, that's all. If a fellow is shaped like a wash-tub, what else could you expect of him when it comes to toting a load of duffle and grub over a Maine carry?"

"And when another angular chap I know is said to resemble a broom-handle, so far as symmetry and plumpness goes, you've got to expect that his greatest feats are accomplished when grub is served. That's a time, Andy Bowles, bugler of the Hampton Troop of Boy Scouts, when you make competition throw up its hands in despair and retire from the field; your capacity in that line is without a peer."

"That's right, Tubby, take a swig of water from your battered old canteen after such a spread-eagle speech. I'm sure your throat must be parched, and as dry as a bone."

"Here, fellows, suppose you let up badgering each other; and after we drop down on this log in the little open glade, what's to hinder us from figuring out our next move in the search for Tubby's Uncle George?"

The energetic speaker was Rob Blake. Those fortunate boys who have read any or all of the preceding volumes in this Series, do not need to be introduced to so prominent a character of the stories; but, of course, there will be many who are making the acquaintance of these wearers of khaki

2

for the first time, and in justice to them it is only fair that we offer a few explanations while the trio stretch themselves upon that friendly pine log.

They all belonged to the famous Eagle Patrol of the Hampton Troop of Boy Scouts, Hampton being a Long Island town on the south shore. In times gone by many were the interesting happenings that came the way of some of the fellows belonging to that patrol. To even enumerate them here would take too long a time, and hence he who is desirous of knowing more about Rob Blake and his chums is referred to earlier volumes, where thrilling and uplifting scenes are depicted in a most entertaining fashion.

Some of these boys had visited the Panama Canal; had even gone abroad and been in a position to witness stirring action in the great war theater of Europe; spent delightful days wandering about the grounds of the wonderful Panama-Pacific Exposition out in California; chased over the torrid deserts of Mexico, when the revolutionist, Pancho Villa, was pursuing his earlier meteor-like career on bloody battlefields; and later still they had been connected with the amazing wave of preparedness that swept over our country from shore to shore. [1]

What brought the three lads far up toward the international border at this season of the fall can be easily explained. As the reader has already learned by reason of the words which Rob Blake uttered when suggesting that they rest from their labors, it had something to do with a relative of fat Tubby Hopkins.

"Uncle George" was a well-to-do gentleman, and a great sportsman. Every autumn he would slip away from business cares and spend a month with a couple of faithful woods guides hunting in the solitudes. Sometimes he went into the "bush" far up in the Canadian wilds after bull moose; or it might be seeking caribou in Labrador. This season it was not so pleasant to be within the boundaries of Canada, owing to the distracted conditions prevailing there, with young fellows enlisting for service abroad, and hundreds of men of German parentage and sympathies held in concentration camps; so Uncle George had wisely chosen to confine his hunting to the most inaccessible region in Maine.

3

Now it chanced that there had been some sort of epidemic in many Long Island communities that summer, and at certain points it held out so long in the fall that the school authorities became alarmed. At Hampton, sessions had been taken up only to be hurriedly discontinued, nor was school to be resumed for a period of at least two weeks.

That gave many of the boys a chance to lay plans for delightful outings. As a rule, the fall was a closed season to them, Saturday being their only off-day; and usually they had to put in most of that weekly holiday practicing for their football games to be played later.

Just at the time this occurred, Tubby Hopkins came to Rob and announced that an opportunity had arisen whereby he and two companions could take a flying trip up into Maine at no cost to themselves, as his father was ready to put up every dollar of the expense.

It seemed that a very important document should be signed by Uncle George within two weeks, or he and Mr. Hopkins stood to lose a large amount of money. Since the devoted sportsman did not plan to be seen in the realm of civilization under a whole month, and could not be reached by wire or letter, it became absolutely necessary that some messenger find his camp, and bring back the document signed.

Tubby asked Rob to engineer the expedition, for he had the utmost faith in the ability of the acting scout master of the troop. As several other fellows had already made arrangements for the new vacation, it happened that Andy Bowles was invited to make the third of the party.

Now, while Tubby and Andy often "scrapped" so far as a verbal exchange of pleasantries was concerned, they really were exceedingly fond of each other; and so the little party promised to get along very nicely together.

They had made the journey by railroad, leaving the cars at a certain small station, and, taking their packs on their backs, starting out on the strength of the rather uncertain schedule of his expected movements, which Uncle George had left behind at his city house when heading toward the Maine wilderness.

If they did not find him at a certain logging camp, at least they were likely to pick up a clue there as to where he had gone, and thus could follow after him. Rob had intended finding a competent guide, but it chanced that there was an unusually heavy demand for experienced woodsmen that season, and they met with several disappointments, until finally the others had urged Rob to make the plunge himself unattended.

They knew that he could be depended on to lead them safely, for Rob had considerable experience in woodcraft, and, besides this, carried a reliable chart of the region they were traversing.

Accordingly they had set forth valiantly, and at the time we meet them had been tramping for two days. According to Rob's figuring, they must be getting close to the logging camp where, possibly, they would find Uncle George; at the same time he also knew that they were near the International Boundary.

"If you take a look over that way, due north, fellows," Rob was telling the other boys, as they sat there on the log, and pointing as he spoke, "you can see for several miles. Notice that big clump of hemlocks on the rise yonder, along the near horizon? Well, unless I miss my guess, that's Canada!"

"But I don't see the line, Rob," observed Tubby vaguely.

At this remark Andy Bowles burst forth in a laugh.

"Why, listen to the innocent, will you, Rob! Honest, now, I believe Tubby thinks the International Boundary is a real line drawn across the Divide from the Atlantic to the Pacific, to mark the division of Uncle Sam's property from the Dominion of Canada and the Great Northwest Territory!"

"Oh, shucks! Of course I was only joking," stammered the confused Tubby. "So that's Canada, is it, Rob? Almost any old place across the line we'd likely find that conditions resembled Belgium and Northern France somewhat, with young men drilling at every crossroads, artillery companies rushing to stations to be sent across the sea, cavalry horses being herded, cattle slaughtered for meat to keep the army supplied, wheat trains heading toward some Atlantic port to be shipped abroad to feed those millions of fighters. Whee! It's hard to believe that peaceful country over there can be *Canada*!"

"Oh, that's only the border, Tubby, you see," explained Rob, always ready to accommodate. "Farther back I've no doubt all those things are daily taking place, for you know Canada has already sent over three hundred thousand soldiers across the sea to fight for the Cause of Civilization. You and I have been at the front, Tubby, and we know the spirit that animates most of those men among the Allies; also how they expect to stick to their job, now they've begun, until it's finished."

"You mean, do you, Rob," interrupted the listening Andy, who had not had the same good fortune as the others to see some of the fighting across in Belgium and Northern France, "that even while the Dominion is being shaken from east to west, right here along the border it's just as it always was?"

"Well, hardly that," continued the other hastily. "You know there have been all sorts of stories in the papers about plots hatched and engineered in the States by those whose sympathies are with Germany, and who feel furious because of the never-ending trains loaded with munitions, soldiers, food, aeroplane parts, motor trucks, and such things that an army in the field would require—these all heading across Canada, and aiming for the ports where steamers are waiting to carry cargoes to Great Britain. It would make these German sympathizers joyous if only *something* might happen to cut off this endless chain of supplies for the Allies."

"Yes," added Tubby eagerly. "I've read where the folks down in Washington are dreadfully alarmed lest one of these terrible schemes may succeed. You recall how the President enjoined everybody in the States to be strictly neutral, and not to lift a hand toward doing anything that might be reckoned an unfriendly or unneighborly act by the aroused people of Canada? So now the Government on both sides is keeping an extra guard along the border, in order to nip any such black scheme in the bud."

"I've been told that's the case," Rob assured them. The talk went on along the same lines until finally the scout master, jumping up, announced:

"Well, we've rested long enough, I guess! We'd better put our best foot forward if we hope to get anywhere near that logging camp close to the border. So pick up your packs, fellows, and we'll be off!"

6

"Oh, listen to that, would you!" cried Tubby excitedly. "It sounded just like the far-away whistle of a railroad locomotive."

"A good guess, Tubby," chuckled Andy, "because that's just what it was. I half expected you'd ask Rob if it could be the scream of one of those Canadian lynx we've heard tell about are to be found up here."

They were conversing while walking, and once again the whistle sounded. Even Tubby could tell now that it came from the northwest. There was also a faint rumbling sound that indicated the passage of a heavy train over a trestle, miles away.

"Yes, the Great Canadian Railway runs close to the boundary along here somewhere," Rob said, "and I suppose we'll often hear distant whistles, for the traffic at present must be unusually heavy. That's likely a long train filled with grain, and all sorts of valuable supplies that are being sent from the rich Saskatchewan and Alberta country, as an offering from the Canadian Northwest granary. It means another nail in the coffin of the Germans, when it reaches the land across the sea. All day long, and night, too, at intervals, those trains are running, carrying millions and millions of dollars' worth of supplies."

"Huh!" chuckled Tubby, "if a German only chanced to live around here, he'd have to stuff cotton in his ears to shut out the sound; because each rumble of trains would mean to him more trouble for his friends across the sea."

They pushed on for some time. Rob evidently had his plan of campaign well figured out, for he now turned sharply to the left and headed almost due west. Apparently he fancied he was as near the International Boundary as there might be any need of going; and that the lone logging camp must lie farther along the new course.

The startling idea had occurred to Tubby that, all unbeknown to themselves, they might inadvertently stray across the line, and be arrested as invaders, by some of those alert Canadian guards mentioned by Rob. The thought disturbed him considerably, and he was about to speak of it, despite the jeers with which he felt sure Andy would greet the idea, when something else suddenly came to pass that completely put it out of his head.

There was a crashing sound heard close by, a swishing of the undergrowth, and then a bounding object flashed into view, which took on the shape of a two-year-old buck, leaping frantically over logs and bushes, as though possessed. Upon his neck and shoulders the boys glimpsed a strange, mysterious gray hunch!

Upon his shoulders the boys glimpsed a strange, mysterious gray hunch.

CHAPTER II
RUMBLINGS OF COMING TROUBLE

"Oh! Did you see that hump on his back, Rob? What could it have been?" gasped Tubby, gripping the sleeve of the other's khaki coat in his excitement.

"Why, Tubby, don't you know that was the pirate of the northern woods?" cried the equally aroused Andy, who had also been stupefied while the little drama was being enacted, and only recovered the use of his hands, and realized that he was carrying a gun, when the leaping buck had completely vanished from view.

"Do you mean a filibuster?" asked the stout boy incredulously.

"Well, yes; you might call a panther by that name," laughed Rob.

"A panther!" echoed Tubby, thrilled more than ever. "Was that what the bunch across the poor deer's shoulders was, Rob? Oh, to think we didn't get a chance to use a gun and save the noble buck!"

"It all happened too fast for me," admitted Andy dejectedly. "Besides, I don't believe any of us could have hit that crouching beast and not harmed the deer."

"No, that's right, Andy," said Rob convincingly. "After all, we only chanced to see one of the woods tragedies that are taking place right along. Panthers must have meat to live on, and deer are their legitimate prey. That's why there's never a close season on the gray buccaneers, nor on wildcats and wolves."

Tubby did not express any timidity in words, but it might have been noticed how he somehow managed to keep a bit closer to his chums after that. If there were such savage "varmints" at large in the country along the International Boundary, Tubby did not think it wise to take any unnecessary chances; not that he would have admitted being *afraid*, of course; but then, as he always said, he offered a shining mark, because a discriminating beast was sure to pick out a plump morsel when foraging for a dinner, and consequently lucky Andy would get off scot-free.

They continued to walk on in a clump, and chatting as they advanced, though Rob kept his eyes and senses constantly on the alert for signs that would tell him what he wished to know.

"I've heard a lot about the Maine woods, and how all sorts of people manage to get a fair living from them, winter or summer," Tubby was saying later on. "Rob, you know something of such things, because you've been up here before. How about it?"

"It's just as you say," Rob replied. "Thousands on thousands of men find ways to wring a living from Nature's storehouse up here in the great pine forests. I've met some of them personally, and asked questions. I've been told all about the others, and what interesting stunts they do."

"Tell us a little about them, please, Rob?" urged Tubby.

"Well," began the scout leader, always willing to oblige his chums when it was within his power to accommodate, "first of all there are the thousands of guides, both natives and Indians, who in summer take parties along the waterways of Maine in canoes, fishing for trout, bass, or salmon in the countless streams and lakes; and in the fall serve the hunters in their camps, when they are after deer and moose. They go to make up quite a little army in themselves, and their wages amount to many hundreds of thousands of dollars per annum. Next in order and importance, I expect, is the gum-hunter."

"Well, I declare, what is a gum-hunter, anyway, Rob?" demanded the listening Tubby. "I've heard of a gumshoe man; but do hunters go shod that way in the Maine woods?"

That allowed Andy, better posted, to have another little explosion,

"Oh, dear innocent, trusting soul, you'll be the death of me yet!" he gasped, between his fits of laughter. "For pity's sake, Rob, tell him quickly what a gum-hunter is, or he'll surely burst with curiosity."

"You must know, Tubby," said Rob, himself smiling broadly, "that spruce gum is used in immense quantities, not only in the manufacture of chewing gum but for several other purposes.

"It is found here in the pine woods of Maine by expert searchers, who at a certain season of the year go forth and gather their harvest. They probably make good wages at their work, too, or there would not be so many of them keeping at it year after year. Some other time I'll go further into details, and tell you how they find the deposits of gum. Some of them even gash trees, and come back in due season to garner the crystal profits that have exuded from the wounds. But the gum-hunter is only one of many chaps who earn a living in these Maine forests. There is the hoop-hole man you're apt to run across in any section where it happens there's a second-growth crop of ash saplings."

"What does he do, Rob?" asked Tubby.

"He gathers the saplings, and occupies his evenings in camp by splitting and assorting and fastening them in bundles. These are later taken away in bulk. They are intended as hoops for barrels, nail-kegs, and such objects. The hoop man does a cracking big business in season, let me tell you.

"Then there's the man who gets out the poles themselves to be used for various purposes; the fellow who hunts for certain crooked woods calculated to make good boats' knees; the sassafras hunter; the ginseng and other root man, who knows where to pick up a little fortune in discovering patches of wild weeds that possess a marketable value when the roots are dug and properly cured; the herb gatherer; and last but far from least the bee man, who goes about looking for hives of wild bees in hollow tree-tops, so he can gather hundreds of pounds of honey."

Tubby looked helplessly around him.

"Well, well," he was heard to say, "you never would believe fortunes could be dug out of such forlorn-looking woods as these. It's simply wonderful what some men can pick up, when others are as blind as bats in the daytime. I'm going to keep my eyes open. We might run across a diamond field."

"Well, you may mean that as a joke," said Rob, "but rare gems have been found around here, which brings up another calling that some men have followed. That is searching all the streams for mussels, because some pretty valuable fresh-water pearls have been discovered, they say, in Maine bivalves."

"It beats all creation how many sources of revenue a smart man can unearth, if only he keeps his wits about him," remarked Andy, who, apparently, was hearing this last bit of information for the first time. "If this terrible war continues much longer there's likely to be another lot of professionals working industriously up here in the woods of Maine. They'll be the friends of the Central Empires, who want to give Old England and her Colonies a backhanded blow by cutting off the supply of munitions and supplies that keeps on flowing toward the coast day after day."

"Oh, why can't the nations of the Old World keep the peace like it's been kept for a hundred years between Uncle Sam and his big northern neighbor?" sighed the tender-hearted Tubby sincerely. "Here's a boundary of over three thousand miles, and not a single fort to mark the dividing line; whereas over across the water, look at the enormous fortresses France and Belgium and Germany have maintained, though none of the Belgians' stood the awful pounding of those enormous guns brought up by the Kaiser's troops."

"There's a good reason for that, Tubby," explained Rob. "Americans and Canadians speak the same tongue, and as a whole have the same aspirations. They understand each other, you see. It's different over in Europe, where different nations hate like poison. We don't seem to meet with the same measure of success down along our Mexican border, because those greasers never can understand our motives, for we think along entirely opposite lines."

"When are we going to have a great World Peace, and war be abolished?" begged Tubby, almost piteously.

"Search me!" said Andy. "Because I don't believe such a thing ever will be, as long as human nature is like it is; though of course I'd be glad to see it brought about. If the nations of the world could only form some sort of practical union, like that of the States now, and so were bound to keep the peace, it might be done. Happy the man who has a hand in such a vast undertaking. If the chance came to me to handle the steering wheel of such a glorious job, why, I'd feel as lofty as—as that hawk soaring right now away up there in the blue heavens!"

Tubby mechanically followed the extended finger of the speaker, and then uttered a sudden startled cry.

"Hawk!" he ejaculated derisively. "That shows *your* ignorance, Andy. Hawk, do you say? Why, bless your simple and confiding nature, don't you know that object away up near the fleecy white clouds, and heading due north at this minute, is nothing more or less than an *aeroplane*? Rob, am I right?"

Rob was himself staring upward, and he hastened to reply:

"That's just what it is, Tubby. After seeing so many of those mosquitoes of the upper air currents soaring above the hostile armies across the big pond, you are able to tell one the minute you glimpse it. Yes, that's an aeroplane, as certain as that we are standing here gaping up at it. I want you to notice that it's heading directly so as to cross the International Boundary line."

"What does that mean, Rob?" questioned Andy curiously, meanwhile continuing to crane his neck.

"Well, I'm only making a guess," Rob ventured. "The chances are that pilot up yonder may be connected with some vile plot to destroy railroad property in the Dominion of Canada, and is now bent on spying out the land so as to make a chart of the country."

CHAPTER III
BY AEROPLANE ACROSS THE BORDER

When the leader of the Eagle Patrol made this astounding assertion both of his friends betrayed additional interest. Indeed, it was a question whether Andy or Tubby, by the rapt expression on their faces, showed the greater excitement.

Tubby had one great advantage over his comrade. He had been abroad with Rob and Merritt Crawford, and had watched aeroplane pilots, both of the Allies and the Germans, shooting like meteors across the skies, bent on their work of learning what was going on back of the enemy's lines so as to give points to those who handled the monster guns far in the rear, allowing them to drop their shells exactly where most wanted.

"Well, to think of the nerve of that fellow!" exclaimed the indignant Andy. "He snaps his fingers at the proclamation of the President about all true Americans standing for strict neutrality. Why, he's meaning to give those Canucks the best chance ever to protest and claim damages from our Government. Isn't that a fact, Rob?"

"Just what it is, Andy," replied the scout master, watching the course of the small object so far up in the air that it resembled a giant bird.

"If they blow up a bridge, and wreck a train loaded with millions of dollars' worth of stuff, and it's proved that the scoundrels passed over from *our* side of the border, Uncle Sam will have to pay the whole bill?" questioned Tubby, now becoming aroused in turn.

"No doubt of it, if the proof is forthcoming," Rob assured him serenely, since he knew enough of treaties and international law for that.

"Then anything that's done against Canada from our side is really a blow aimed at our own country?" questioned Andy, beginning to show signs of anger. "Why, if it stands that way, then those conspirators are just as bad as if they were trying to knock a big hole in the U. S. Treasury, from which untold oodles of money could drop out. They're breaking the neutrality laws smack. I'd like to let 'em know just what I think of such sneaks. There ought to be some way to detect and punish such backhanded knockers."

"Oh, there are plenty of ways!" asserted Rob. "The law is stern enough, if you only can catch them in the act. There's the rub. They take all sorts of precautions to hide their identity. Who could recognize that chap up a mile or so from the earth? How does any one know that he's meaning to drop lower presently, so as to take a lot of pictures of the railroad where it passes over a bridge or trestle?"

"Is *that* the way it's done?" ejaculated the deeply interested Andy, who was more or less ignorant of how air pilots make themselves so useful in war times.

"Watch him!" snapped Rob, and all eyes were again focussed on the far distant object moving across the heavens, and passing some fleecy fragment of a floating white cloud.

"As sure as anything he's dropping on a regular toboggan slant!" cried Andy, thrilled by the sight.

"Huh!" remarked the wise Tubby, with the pride of superior knowledge, "that's what they call volplaning. Sometimes an aviator will shoot down for a mile like a streak of lightning, and just when you think he must be smashed against the ground he'll suddenly stop, just like a descending eagle does, and sail away as nice as you please on a lower level."

"Which is exactly what that spy is doing right now!" exclaimed Andy. "I guess he is down far enough for him to see all he wants to, and also snap off some pictures. But, Rob, if there are Canadian troops guarding the bridge across there why wouldn't they give him a volley to let him know he hadn't any business on that side of the International Line?"

"I expect that's what they will do any minute now," Rob assured him. "We may not hear the sound of the guns over here; miles lie between; but we ought to be able to tell by the actions of the aviator. If the lead commences to sing about his ears, he's likely to mount again; he'll be afraid of having his gasolene tank pierced by one of them, or be struck himself."

"When we were on the other side, Rob," interjected Tubby,

"you know we always said petrol instead of gasolene; but they both mean the same thing. There, look, will you; he's started up again, as sure as anything, making spirals, as they generally do when ascending in a big hurry."

As Tubby declared, the man in the aeroplane had suddenly changed his location and was now ascending as fast as he could. Something had undoubtedly caused him to do this. Rob said he wished he had thought to fetch a pair of binoculars along with him, for then they might see spurts of smoke on the ground, and possibly even discover the bridge itself.

"But then who would ever dream we'd want glasses for such a purpose?" Tubby observed. "Goodness knows we're lugging enough load as it is. He is turning around now, Rob, and heading this way again. Do you think he accomplished his purpose, and is now bent on getting out of range of those bullets?"

"Very likely," the other replied, "though his danger was more imaginary than real. To strike a moving aeroplane at that height with an ordinary military rifle would be next door to an accident. Haven't we seen air pilots take all sorts of daring chances, with shrapnel bursting all around them?"

The three scouts watched until the mysterious machine had vanished toward the south. They could hear the sound of the motor as it passed high overhead, though at a considerably lower level than when going the other way.

Once more then they started off, though Tubby had great difficulty in "getting a move on him," as he called it; for that load on his back seemed to make him feel like Sinbad the Sailor when the Old Man of the Sea refused to dismount from his shoulders, after being assisted along the way, demanding that he be carried still farther.

The afternoon was now beginning to wane very fast. Already the westering sun had sunk far down in the heavens, and was heading for the horizon. While their conversation had been mostly upon the entrancing topic of that strict neutrality which had been enjoined on all citizens of the United States while the World War was in progress across the sea, at the same time Tubby's thoughts would frequently stray to his own present troubles.

"It doesn't look much like we would run across that old logging camp to-day, where Uncle George was going to make his first stay, does it, Rob?" he was heard to ask for possibly the sixth time.

And as he had patiently done on every other occasion the scout leader answered him pleasantly.

"I'm sorry to say there's little chance of that happening, Tubby, much as all of us would like it. According to my rough chart, we must be getting in the neighborhood of that camp, though, and, if lucky, we might even run across your uncle to-morrow. Certainly, if we hear any shooting near by we'll give a shout, and try to find out who's who. That's the best I can say, Tubby."

"Thank you, Rob, very much," said the fat boy sweetly. "I know well enough that if it depended on you we'd arrive in camp inside of half an hour. Then, having accomplished my mission up here, we could all give ourselves up to a delightful ten days of knocking around, and doing some hunting with his guides. That means we'll soon have to call a halt ourselves and camp?"

Rob had to laugh at the vein of pleading he could detect in Tubby's voice when he made that apparently innocent remark.

"I'm looking around for a good site, Tubby," he announced, and at that the moon face of the stout member of the patrol fairly beamed with pleasure.

It was not more than ten minutes afterward when Rob stopped short.

"Here's where we spend the night, fellows," he told them.

"A bully good place," assented Andy, casting a look of appreciation around at the trees, with several openings that allowed them to see the sky, and gave a promise of all the fresh air they would want.

"Yes, and I hear a brook gurgling along near by!" declared Tubby;—"the main reason why you picked out this place, Rob. The water left in my canteen is getting pretty stale, so I'll be mighty glad to get a decent cool drink of sweet water."

He hastily slipped out of the broad bands of his pack, and

17

scurried over in the direction whence that pleasing drip of water was heard. The others saw him stop and then lie flat on his paunch, for with Tubby it was not so easy to get his mouth down to a low level, owing to his peculiar formation; usually his heels had to be higher than his head, just as you would tilt a barrel up to make the rim come in contact with the ground, all owing to that curve of the staves.

As they carried no tent, for that was utterly out of the question, it would be necessary for the trio of scouts to make some apology for a shelter calculated to keep the dew or the frost from chilling their bodies, as they slept in the open.

But, indeed, this was only a delight to these lads, accustomed as all of them were to roughing it. Many a time in the past had they constructed a brush shanty that, in an emergency, might even shed rain to some extent, and would surely afford them shelter from the chilly night air.

All of them got busy immediately, fetching branches and every manner of material that would be needed in the task. While Rob himself took over the job of building the shack, he had Andy cutting wood for a fire, and Tubby dragging further supplies of fuel toward the spot, so that altogether it made quite an animated picture, with everybody working like beavers.

Before the evening was fully upon them, things began to take on quite a homelike appearance. The shanty was completed, being rudely built, with a decided slant toward the back, and an open front. Some sportsmen's tents are made on the same pattern, the idea being to have the fire so placed as to cause the sloping roof to reflect the heat that comes in through the open front.

Then came the always delightful job of cooking supper. No boy was ever known to object to lending a hand when this task is broached. Tubby, being something of a chef by this time, due to a grim determination to excel in one branch, even if he could never equal Rob in woodcraft knowledge, or other fellows in their several fads, had taken it upon himself to carry out the arrangements.

His depression had fled. The other boys were so full of optimism that it seemed to fill the air, even as that tempting smell of coffee, with fried onions, potatoes and bacon as accessories did. A more despondent chap than Tubby must have yielded to the general feeling of satisfaction.

Witness them, therefore, a little later on, spread out close to the fire, each with his legs crossed under him tailor-fashion, and bent on stowing away the heaping pannikin of hot food that had been served out as his share of the supper; while the big tin cups were brimming full of fragrant coffee that, as Andy said, "went straight to the spot every time."

The first edge of their ferocious appetites appeased, the boys did not hurry, but took their time in eating. It was that delightful hour of the early evening in the pine woods when all Nature seems to be hushed, and the heart of the camper rejoices in his surroundings, which he joyously compares with the unhappy lot of those mortals who are compelled to remain amidst the skyscrapers of the city, chained to their desks, while the camper owns the whole world.

CHAPTER IV
AN INVASION OF THE CAMP

"Rob," remarked Andy, later on, "why would those plotters choose Maine as the field for their dastardly attempts to strike at the Canadian Government? I should think they would have a bigger chance for succeeding in their undertaking, say away up in the Northwest, where the border isn't watched as closely as along here."

"That's easy to answer," replied the scout master. "In the first place you must remember that as all these supplies gathered through the Great Northwest granary approach the coast, where they are to be shipped abroad, they concentrate. It's like the spokes of a wheel, and this eastern stretch of country can be likened to the hub. Get that, Andy?"

"I certainly do, Rob. This applies, I suppose, to some extent with regard to the soldiers, and the munitions, and all that; they are gathered here and there, and as the many rivulets draw closer to the coast the stream grows larger all the while. Sure, that stands to reason, and I was silly not to think of it myself."

"Another thing that counts heavily," added Rob sagely, "is the fact that out in the Northwest that you mention the transcontinental railroad doesn't come anywhere as near the border as it does close to the Maine line. So, you see, an expedition crossing over here would have only a short distance to go before they reached the tracks they meant to destroy."

"Yes," said Tubby, who had been listening eagerly, "and perhaps there's a bridge here that, if blown up, would about paralyze the stream of material that's flowing steadily down toward the coast day after day. I reckon it's to stop that tide of munitions and supplies, as much as the soldiers themselves, that these fellows are scheming to do."

"There's another far-off whistle of a train," said Andy, perking his head up in a listening attitude. "They certainly come along quite frequently, and that goes to tell what a big business is being done by the railroad these days. I understand thousands of horses are being shipped from the ranches up on those big prairies of the Canadian Northwest, for they last only a short time in war, and the supply is beginning to fall short. Already I've read how the rival armies are making great powerful tractor engines take the place of animals in dragging heavy guns to the front."

"Supposing that air pilot did succeed in getting all the information needed," Tubby went on to say, "as well as some pretty smart pictures of the ground around the bridge, how soon would those plotters start to work, do you reckon, Rob? Surely not this very night?"

"Well, hardly, Tubby," came the reassuring answer, "though we can't say what need of haste there might be. If the aviator did snap off some pictures, the film would have to be developed, and prints made, which takes time. No, at the earliest I should say to-morrow night would be picked out for the attempt."

"Oh, well, the guards are on duty, and are looking out for anything of that kind," said Andy carelessly. "The visit from that aeroplane will put them on their mettle."

"Unless," Rob ventured thoughtfully, "they considered that the pilot was merely some venturesome American who had taken chances in crossing the boundary air, and found himself over Canada. It might be their shots were only sent to warn him he had better clear out, and to mind his own business."

"Whee! In that case they might be caught napping," said Tubby, with a vein of anxiety in his voice. "Rob, would it be any business of ours to warn the Canadians guarding the trestle or bridge, if we had the chance?"

"It would be our patriotic *duty*, if we really knew that mischief was brooding," the scout master told him sternly. "Stop and think for a minute, and you'll see it in that way too. First of all, as true scouts, we would have to consider that these men, no matter how much they loved the land of their birth across the sea, are either citizens of the United States, or even if Germans, are enjoying the hospitality of Uncle Sam. To creep across the line so as to strike at their foe would be to

21

abuse that hospitality. Yes, it would be the duty of any honest, patriotic American citizen to give warning, if he absolutely knew that such a scheme was afoot."

"Do you mean to carry the news to some town in Maine, from where it could be wired to Washington, so that soldiers might be sent up here to frustrate the evil designs of these schemers?" asked Tubby, who at times delighted in framing his questions in exceedingly weighty language.

Rob Blake reflectively rubbed his chin as he considered this query.

"I'm afraid that would consume far too much time, Tubby," he finally replied. "Before those troops could be rushed here from the nearest army post the mischief, such as it was, would have been carried through. No; if I learned positively that those German sympathizers meant to invade Canada, something the same way as the Fenians did a long time ago, I'd consider it my bounden duty to cross the line myself and try and warn the guards at the bridge."

"That's the ticket, Rob!" cried the delighted Andy, who himself believed in "hitting the nail on the head." Tubby, a bit slower to grasp possibilities, bent closer, the better to hear what was said.

Much more was spoken of along these lines, but the reader has already learned what the boys, as young American patriots, were bent on doing should the occasion arise, and hence it is not necessary to repeat all that passed between them.

Of course they also talked of other things, returning to this fascinating theme from time to time. Often Tubby stared in the direction of the North Star, in company with the Great Bear or Dipper constellation; and at these times his round, rosy face registered an expression of awe. Tubby might have been gifted with a sense of second sight, and dimly may have seen possible complications they were fated soon to meet.

As the evening grew, all of them felt an inclination to turn in. They had covered many miles, and not over level ground, since the morning, and with those heavy packs on their backs it had proved to be quite a tiresome journey.

Tubby, in particular, was yawning terrifically, nor did he take the trouble to put his hand over his extended jaws. Often Andy would pretend to shudder, and warn him to be more careful, or both of his chums would fall into the huge opening.

Tubby would make no reply; he was too sleepy to enter into any argument. He may have had an object in his repeated yawning, knowing how contagious it is, and that presently he was bound to start both the others along similar lines.

Presently Rob was seen to copy his example. Andy followed suit.

"Guess we might as well turn in," said the latter, with a grin, as he caught the eye of Tubby on him. "Tubby here will surely fall to pieces unless he gets some sleep."

"Huh!" grunted Tubby scornfully. "Now that you've begun, too, Andy, and Rob gives like signs, we'll be making it unanimous. What about the fire, though? Do we let that cheery blaze die out during the night?"

"No need of that," said Rob immediately. "It promises to be pretty chilly, and our blankets aren't any too thick at that; so I plan to get up once in a while and throw an armful of wood on the fire. If I don't oversleep I think I can keep the thing going up to morning. Andy, if you chance to wake up any time, and find that the fire has got down to red ashes, you might crawl out and take a turn. Plenty of fuel handy, you know."

"I'll try and remember, Rob," promised the other, "though I must say I do sleep as sound as a top. If you depended on me to attend to the fire the chances are it would expire long before dawn. But I may wake up once or twice, and I'll do my duty, Rob, only too gladly. Pile in, Tubby. Your blanket is over there on the left of the entrance, and we'd have a nice time of it letting *you* crawl over us."

Rob did not follow immediately, for he was busying himself at the fire. They were careful to take their belongings into the brush shanty with them, except certain things that could just as well hang high from a limb of the tree. There was no sign of rain or snow, so that they did not worry on that score.

Finally Rob came crawling inside the shelter. He fancied that one or both of his chums might already have dropped asleep, and did not mean to do anything to disturb them. Yes, he could hear Tubby's heavy breathing, which announced that the stout boy had drifted across the border of slumberland and was perhaps already dreaming of Hampton folks, or some past scenes in his ambitious career as a scout.

"He's off, Rob," Andy remarked in a low voice. "Gee! but Tubby can go to sleep the easiest of any one I ever knew. Honest, now, I believe he could take a nap while walking along, if only some fellows kept him from tumbling over. All he has to do is to shut his eyes, take half a dozen long breaths, and then he's clear gone."

"Well, don't talk any more now, Andy. We'll both try to imitate his sensible example," cautioned the other, as he started to creep under his blanket, having removed his shoes and coat beforehand, although he wisely kept them handy in case a sudden necessity should arise.

So the time passed. Rob did wake up some hours afterward, and creeping out replenished the fire. As he did so he took note of the fact that once again there faintly came to his ears the long-drawn whistle of an engine; and he fancied that it meant to notify those who guarded the bridge of the approach of a fresh train loaded with valuable army stores, or troops bound for the war trenches over in Northern France.

Again Rob snuggled down under his blanket, feeling grateful for the comforts that a generous fortune had supplied him with. He was not long in going to sleep.

Happily no one was nervous in that camp. He, too, soon lost consciousness, and possibly slept for several hours, for when next he awoke the fire had once more died down to red embers.

This time, however, the awakening was along entirely different lines. It was caused by the whole end of their brush shanty falling down with a crash, as though some heavy object had been hurled against it. At the same time the startled trio of scouts, sitting hastily up amidst the wreckage of their late shelter, saw some huge lumbering object scatter the glowing embers of the smouldering fire in every direction as it dashed madly through the camp.

Tubby was stricken dumb with amazement. Possibly he had been indulging in some extravagant dream in which the giant Jabberwock that sported through "Alice in Wonderland" was creating great excitement. He stared at the vanishing bulky animal as though he could hardly believe his eyes. Andy apparently had not lost control of his vocal organs, to judge by the shout he let out.

CHAPTER V
COMFORTING TUBBY

"Hey! What does this mean, knocking our house to flinders that way? Hold up, you, and tell us what you're aiming at. A nice old farm bull you are, to be treating strangers so rough! Say, look at the dead leaves catching on fire, will you, boys!"

"Get busy, everybody!" called out Rob, already commencing to pull his shoes on as fast as he could, so that he might creep out from the wreckage of the brush shanty and prevent a forest fire from starting.

Andy followed suit. Tubby, not having been wise enough to keep his footwear close to his hand, had some difficulty in finding his shoes. Consequently when he did finally emerge, looking like a small edition of an elephant down on its knees, he found that the others had succeeded in gathering the scattered firebrands together again, and that some fresh pine was already flaming up, so dispelling the darkness.

Indeed, the growing warmth of the resurrected fire did not feel disagreeable in the least, for the night air was exceedingly chilly.

"Great Jupiter! Was that really a Jabberwock?" demanded Tubby, when he joined the other pair by the fire, holding out his chubby hands to the warmth as if the sensation felt very good.

"It was a bull moose," replied Rob, without a moment's hesitation.

"But what ailed the critter," demanded Andy, "to make such a savage attack on our brush shanty, and dash through the half-dead fire like he did? That's what I'd like to know. Rob, does a bull moose do such things always?"

"I'm sure I can't say," replied the other. "They are stupid creatures, I've always heard, and apt to do all sorts of queer stunts. It may be one of the animals could be taken with a mad streak, just as I've read a rhinoceros will do, charging down on a hunter's camp, and smashing straight through the white tent as if he felt he had a special grievance against it. All I know is, that was an old bull moose, for I saw his big clumsy horns."

Tubby shook his head, not yet convinced, and mumbled:

"I never saw a Jabberwock. I'm not sure there is any such strange beast in the world, but that didn't resemble what I thought a moose was like."

"You'll have to prove it to him, Rob," ventured Andy, "for when Tubby doubts he is like a wagon stuck in the mud: it takes a mighty heave to pry him loose."

Thereupon Rob leaned forward and taking up a blazing brand that would serve admirably as a torch, he walked around until he found what he was looking for.

"Come here, both of you, and take a look at this track," he told them.

"Huh! Looks like the spoor of a farmyard cow, only bigger. The cleft in the hoof is there, all right; so if a moose really did make that track, as you say, Rob, then they must belong to the same family of the cloven hoofs."

"Here's another bit of evidence, you see," continued Rob, bent on rubbing it in while about the matter. "In passing under this tree the animal must have scraped his back pretty hard. Here's a wad of dun-colored hair clinging to this branch. That proves it to be a moose, Tubby."

"What if the old rascal should take a sudden notion to make another savage attack on our camp?" suggested Andy. "Hadn't we better get ready to give him a warm reception, Rob? The law is up on moose and deer now, I believe. I'd like to drop that old sinner in his tracks. I'm going to get my gun."

"No harm in being ready, Andy, though there's small chance of his returning," Rob replied. He, too, crept over to where his rifle lay, and secured the weapon. "His fury expended itself in that mad rush, I reckon. He would never dare attack us while the fire is jumping up."

Nevertheless, the trio sat there for some time on guard. Andy, with the plea for neutrality still before his mind, and recent events down along the Mexican border, as read in the daily papers, occurring to him, called it "watchful waiting."

"But what are we going to do for a shelter?" bleated Tubby finally, as if once more finding the temptation to sleep overpowering him.

"Oh, we'll have to do without, and make the fire take the place of a brush covering," remarked Andy superciliously, as became an old and hardened hunter. "Why, many times I've wrapped myself in a blanket, and with my feet to the blaze slept like a rock! I wonder what time it is now?"

While Andy was feeling around for his nickel watch, Rob shot a quick look overhead, to note the position of certain of the planets, which would give him the points he wanted to know.

"Close to three, I should say," he hazarded, and presently Andy, on consulting his dollar timepiece, uttered an exclamation of wonder.

"Why, Rob, you're a regular wizard!" he broke out with. "It's that hour exactly. If you had eyes that could see into my pocket like the wonderful Roentgen rays, you couldn't have hit it closer. I guess you know every star up there, and just where they ought to be at certain times."

"It's easy enough to get the time whenever you can see certain stars," explained the scout leader modestly, "though you wouldn't hit it so exactly very often as I did then. But as there are some three and a half hours before dawn comes we might as well soak in a little more of that good sleep."

He showed Tubby how to arrange his blanket, and even tucked him in carefully, with his head away from the fire.

"You're a mighty good fellow, Rob," muttered Tubby sleepily, and they heard no more from him until hours had expired and morning was at hand.

There was no further alarm. The singular old bull moose must have wandered into other pastures after that mad break. They neither saw nor heard him again. It was just as well for the same Mr. Moose that he decided not to repeat his escapade, since he might not have gotten off so cleverly the next time, with those scouts on the alert, and their weapons handy for immediate service.

With the coming of morning the three boys awoke, and quickly prepared breakfast. Rob did not mean to go very far on that day. He believed that according to his chart and the verbal information he had received, they were in the immediate vicinity of the deserted logging camp near the border. He intended to circle around a bit, looking for signs that would lead them to it. All the while they could also keep on the alert for any rifle-shot that would indicate the presence of hunters in the neighborhood.

"There's that railway whistle again," remarked Andy, pausing while in the act of turning a flapjack, in the making of which he professed to be singularly adroit, so that he seldom lost a chance to mix up a mess for breakfast when the others would allow him.

"Guess the trains must have been passing all through the night, even if I didn't hear any," confessed Tubby frankly.

"Do you know, fellows," asked Andy, since confession seemed to rule the hour, "the first thought that flashed through my head when we were so suddenly aroused in the night by all that row, was that the bridge had been dynamited by the German sympathizers, and the guards shot up sky-high with it. Of course, I quickly realized my mistake as soon as I glimpsed that pesky old moose lighting out, with the red embers of our fire scattered among all the dead leaves, and a dozen little blazes starting up like fun."

"I wonder has any forest fire ever started in that same way?" ventured Tubby.

"If you mean through a crazy bull moose ramming through a bed of hot ashes," Andy told him, "I don't believe it ever did. For all we know no moose ever carried out such a queer prank before last night; even if such a thing happened, why the hunters would put the fire out, just as we did."

"I guess Uncle George would have been tickled to see a big moose at close quarters like that," said Tubby. "He's shot one a year for a long while past. He stops at that, because he says they're getting thinned out up here in Maine, and even over in Canada, too."

Breakfast over, the boys loitered around for a while. None of them seemed particularly anxious to be on the move, Andy feeling indifferent, Rob because he knew they were not going far that day, and Tubby through an aversion to once more shouldering that heavy pack. In truth, the only gleam of light that came to Tubby he found in the fact that each day they were bound to diminish their supply of food, and thus the burden would grow constantly lighter.

Finally Rob said they had better be making a start.

"Understand, boys," he told them, with a smile, "we needn't try for a record to-day. The fact is, I have reason to believe that old deserted logging camp must be somewhere around this very spot. So, instead of striking away toward the west, we'll put in our time searching for signs to lead us to it. At any minute we may run across something like a trail, or a grown-up tote-road, along which we can make our way until we strike the log buildings where Uncle George said he meant to make his first stop."

"Oh! thank you for saying that, Rob," Tubby burst out with, as his face radiated his happy state of mind. "For myself I wouldn't mind if we just stuck it out here for a whole week, and let Uncle George find us. But then that wouldn't be doing the right by my father, so we'll have to keep on hunting."

"I don't mean to get much further away from the boundary," continued Rob, "for what we saw yesterday bothers me. There's certainly some desperate scheme brooding; that's as plain as anything to me."

"Just to think," said Tubby, looking around him with a trace of timidity on his ruddy face and in his round eyes, "we may be close to a nest of terrible schemers who mean to do something frightfully wicked, and get poor old Uncle Sam in a hole with the Canadian authorities. Rob, supposing this job is pulled off, and those Canadians feel mighty bitter over the breach of neutrality, do you think they'd march right down to Washington and demand satisfaction? I heard you say they had raised a force of three hundred thousand and more drilled men, and that beats our regular army."

"I guess there's small chance of such a thing happening, Tubby," laughed Andy. "You can let your poor timid soul rest easy. In the first place nearly all the three hundred thousand men have already been sent across the ocean to fight the Germans in the French war trenches, or else they are drilling in England. Then again our cousins across the border are far too sensible."

"Don't worry about that a minute," he was told. "What we must keep in mind is that our patriotism may be called on to prevent these men from breaking our friendly relations with our neighbor, that have stood the test of time so well. If only we could find your Uncle George, Tubby, we'd put it up to him what ought to be done."

"But even if we don't run across him," ventured Tubby bravely, "I guess we're capable as scouts of taking such a job in hand of our own accord; yes, and carrying it through to a successful culmination."

"Hear! hear!" said Andy, who liked to listen to Tubby when the latter showed signs of going into one of his periodical spasms of "spread-eagleism" as the thin scout was wont to call these flights of oratory.

So the morning passed away, and while they had not covered a great extent of territory by noon, at least the boys had kept up a persistent search for signs that would tell of the presence near by of the abandoned logging camp.

CHAPTER VI
THE LOGGING CAMP

It was along toward the middle of the day when Rob announced welcome news. He called a halt, and as the other pair stood at attention the scout master turned on Tubby with a look that thrilled the stout chum exceedingly.

"What is it, Rob?" he gasped, the perspiration streaming down his fat cheeks in little rivulets, for the day had grown a bit warm after that chilly night. "I know, you've run across signs at last?"

"Speak up, Rob, and give us a hint, please," urged the hardly less impatient Andy.

"I wanted to see if you fellows were using your eyes, first," explained Rob; "but Tubby seemed to be searching his inward soul for something he had lost; and, well, I imagine Andy here was figuring on what he wanted for his next meal, because neither one of you at this minute has thought it worth while to take a good look down at your feet. Right now you're standing on the sign!"

They began to cast their eyes earthward. Andy almost immediately burst out with:

"Whee! an old long-disused tote-road, as the lumbermen call the track where the logs are dragged to the rivers, to be later on put behind a boom, and wait for the regular spring rise! Am I correct, Rob?"

"Straight as a die, Andy; this is a tote-road," replied Rob.

"But what good is that going to do us, I'd like to know?" ventured Tubby, groping as usual for an explanation. "We don't want to go to any river, that I know of. What we're itching to find is the logging camp."

"This track is going to bring us to it, sooner or later," asserted Rob, with conviction in his tones. "I can give a pretty good guess which way the logs were taken along here, from the signs that are left on the trees and the bushes. Anybody with half a mind could tell that much. Very well, we must follow the track back, and keep watch for another road showing where the horses were daily taken to their sheds at the camp. I imagine it's going to be a simple enough solution to the puzzle, boys."

Andy was delighted. Tubby, having been convinced that the leader knew what he was talking about, managed to enthuse. Truth to tell, Tubby was yearning for the delightful minute to arrive when he might toss down that heavy pack of his for good and all, since they expected to go out of the pine woods much lighter than they came in.

They determined to sit down and eat a bite of lunch. After that they would again take up their task, the rainbow of promise glowing in the sky ahead of them.

"Have we gone a great distance away from the border, do you think, Rob?" Andy was asking, while they devoured such food as could be prepared quickly over a small fire.

"Well, that's something I can't exactly say yes or no to," came the answer. "I don't know where the dividing line comes. According to my reckoning we ought to be about as close as we were last night. In fact, I should say we are now exactly opposite the long bridge over on the Canadian side of the border."

"But how could that be, Rob, when we've been doing considerable walking since breaking camp this morning?" demanded Tubby incredulously, but more as a means for increasing his stock of information than because he entertained the least doubt concerning the statement made.

"Our tramping hasn't covered over half a mile in a direct line, because we went over a zigzag course," replied the leader. "If you remember, whenever we heard a whistle for the bridge, it came from the west, showing that the structure lay farther that way."

"Sure, you're on the job when you say that, Rob!" exclaimed Andy, who had been an interested listener. "Only twenty minutes ago we all heard a rumbling sound, and decided it was made by a long freight train passing over the trestle leading to the bridge. It came from a point exactly opposite to us. You wouldn't want any better proof than that, Tubby."

33

So they chatted, and ate, and passed half an hour. Then Rob said it would be well if they once more went forth. That tote-road was an alluring object to Rob; he wanted to prove his theory a true one.

Once more they began to "meander," as Tubby called it, through the woods, which had begun to thin out considerably, since most of the better trees had been cut down years back, and in places the ground was almost impassable with the wreckage of dead branches. Fortunately no fire had ever run through this region to complete the devastation begun by the axes of the lumbermen.

It could not have been more than half an hour later when Rob announced that he had discovered where the horses were in the habit of leaving the tote-road and following a well-defined trail through the brush and scant trees.

"Keep a lookout for the camp, fellows!" he told them, whereat Tubby began to elevate his head and sniff the air with vehemence.

"I thought I caught a whiff of pine-smoke," he said, "but I must have been mistaken. Still, as the air is in our faces, it wouldn't be strange if we did get our first indication of the presence of the lumber camp through our well developed sense of smell, rather than by reason of our eyesight."

"Wrong again, Tubby," chuckled Andy. "Eyes have it this time; there's your camp ahead of us. Look over the top of that clump of brush, you'll see the flat roof of a long log shanty, which must be the bunk-house of the lumber jacks in the days when they spent a winter here chopping."

Even Tubby agreed with Andy after he had shaded his eyes with his hand and taken a square look. The thought that they were finally at the end of their search for Uncle George was very pleasing, and Tubby laughed as though a tremendous load had already been taken from his shoulders.

"Why, it wasn't such a great task after all," he remarked, as though he had never once dreamed of being despondent.

"Wait," cautioned Rob. "Don't count your chickens before they are hatched, Tubby. It's poor policy to be too sanguine."

"But Rob, didn't you just say that was the camp?" pleaded the other.

"No doubt about it, Tubby. But possibly the person we're wanting to interview may not be in the place," reminded the scout master.

"What makes you say that, Rob?"

"Oh! I've got a sort of suspicion that way," responded Rob. "In the first place we haven't heard a single gunshot since arriving in the vicinity of this place yesterday, and that alone looks queer. Then we can see the roof of the bunk-house, with the mud and slat chimney in plain sight; it's after the noon hour, too, and the chances are there'd be more or less cooking going on if the place were occupied, but so far as I can make out not the faintest trace of smoke is flowing from that homely chimney."

Tubby, staring hard again, saw the truth of these assertions. He heaved a heavy sigh and shook his head dismally.

"Tough luck, I should call it, if Uncle George has never been here at all, and ours is going to be a regular wild-goose chase. Whichever way can we turn, Rob?"

"There you go jumping at conclusions, hand over fist, Tubby," said Andy quickly. "Rob doesn't mean that at all. Why, stop and think how your uncle was so very particular to mention that communications of importance sent to this camp would get to him in due time. He's handling some big business, and couldn't afford to drop out of the world entirely, even for two weeks. If he's left here be sure we'll find something to tell us where to look for him."

"Come along and let's see," urged Tubby, "they say the proof of the pudding lies in the eating. Inside of five minutes or so we ought to know the worst, or the best. I'll try and stand the shock, fellows."

Once more they advanced. They could not always keep in a direct line on account of the obstacles that beset their course, so that Tubby's estimate of the time required to reach the deserted logging camp proved erroneous; but by the end of ten minutes the little party drew up before the door of the long cabin which they understood had once sheltered a score of those rough wielders of the ax known as lumberjacks.

Some of the other rude buildings constituting the "camp" were in various stages of decay and in tumble-down ruin, but the bunk-house seemed to have been more substantially built, for it looked as though intact.

Before they arrived all of the boys had made a discovery that increased their haste to reach the door. There was some sort of paper fastened to it, and Rob had a pretty good idea as to what it would turn out to be.

"Uncle George has gone away from here, and left directions where to look for him," announced Andy promptly, showing that he, too, had made a guess concerning the nature of that notice on the door.

"Shucks!" Tubby was heard to grunt, at the same time giving his burden an impatient flirt, as though almost in a humor to rebel against another long siege of packing it over miles and miles of dreary pineland.

But a surprise, and a pleasing one at that, awaited them all as they found themselves able to decipher the writing on the paper.

It proved to be a business sheet, with Uncle George's printed address up in the left-hand corner. He himself had written the message in a bold hand, which any one capable of reading at all might easily make out; and this was what the trio of scouts read:

NOTICE.

"We have gone over to the Tucker Pond to try again for the big moose that for two past seasons has managed to fool me. This year I hope to bag him. He is a rare giant in size. Make yourselves at home. The latch string is always out. We expect to be back in a few days at the most. The door is only barred on the outside. Enter, and wait, and make merry.

(Signed)
"George Luther Hopkins."

When Tubby read that delightful news he fell to laughing

until he shook like a bowlful of jelly. It evidently made him very happy, and he did not hesitate to show it to his two faithful comrades. Indeed, all of them had smiles on their faces, for it would be much more satisfactory to loaf around this spot, possibly taking toll of the partridges, and perhaps even a wandering deer, than to continue their search for an elusive party, whose movements might partake of the nature of a will-o'-the-wisp.

"I'm going to make a sign reading 'Alabama,' and stick it above the door, the first thing," announced Tubby, with a grateful heart. "It means 'here we rest.' If ever three fellows deserved a spell of recuperation we certainly are those fellows."

"How generous of Uncle George," said Andy, "to say the latch string is always out! Then, too, he calls attention to the fact that the door is only held shut by a bar on the outside, instead of within. All we have to do, fellows, is to drop our packs here. I'll remove that bar, and swing the door wide open, after which we'll step in and take possession."

He proceeded to follow out this nice little program,—at least he got as far as dropping his pack and removing the bar; but hardly had he started to open the door than Andy gave a sudden whoop, and slammed it shut again with astonishing celerity. Tubby and Rob stared at him as though they thought he had seen a genuine ghost.

CHAPTER VII
AN UNWELCOME INTRUDER

"Oh! what did you see inside the cabin, Andy?" gasped Tubby, beginning to look alarmed, and shrinking back a little, because he did not happen to be carrying one of the two guns in the party.

"Wow! Talk to me about your Jabberwock!" ejaculated Andy, making his face assume an awed expression that added to Tubby's state of dismay. "He's in there!"

"But how could a big bull moose get inside a cabin, when the door's shut, and fastened with a bar?" questioned the amazed and incredulous fat scout.

"It isn't any moose," scoffed Andy, and, turning to Rob, he went on: "I tell you, the biggest bobcat I ever set eyes on is in there, and has been having a high old time scratching around among the provisions left by Uncle George and his party. Oh, his yellow eyes looked like balls of phosphorus in the half gloom. I thought he was going to jump for me, so I slammed the door shut, and set the bar again."

"A wildcat, do you say?" observed Rob, looking decidedly interested. "Well, one thing sure, Uncle George never meant that generous invitation for this destructive creature. As he couldn't very well read the notice, or lift that heavy bar, it stands to reason the cat found some other way of entering the bunk-house."

"How about the chimney, Rob?" asked Andy, as quick as a flash.

"Now I wouldn't be much surprised if that turned out to be his route," mused the scout leader. "They have a wonderful sense of smell, you know, and this fellow soon learned that there were things good to eat inside the cabin. Finding the place deserted, so far as his two-footed enemies were concerned, he must have prowled all around, and finally mounted to the roof. Then the opening in the chimney drew his attention, and getting bolder as time passed, he finally dropped down."

Tubby, who had been listening with rapt attention, now broke out again.

"He must be a mighty bold cat to do that, I should say, fellows. Goodness knows how much damage he's done to Uncle George's precious stores. Oh! doesn't it seem like a shame to have a miserable pussycat spoiling the stuff you've gone and nearly broken your back to pack away up here? But will we have to pitch a camp in one of those other smaller buildings, and let the bobcat hold the fort in the comfortable bunkhouse, with its jolly cooking fireplace?"

Thereupon Andy snorted in disdain.

"I'd like to see myself doing that cowardly thing, Tubby!" he exclaimed. "Possession may be nine points of the law, but in this case there's something bigger than the law, and that's self-preservation. That beast is going to pay for his meddling, if I know what's what. Rob, how'd we better go at the job?"

"Just as you said a while back, Andy," the scout master told him, "the hand of every man is always raised against such varmints in the woods as panthers and bobcats and weasels and such animals as destroy heaps of game, both in the fur and in the feather. If I could have shot that panther without harming the deer I'd have been only too pleased to do it; but the whole thing happened too rapidly for us. As to just what our plan of campaign now ought to be, that's worth considering."

They had deposited their bundles on the ground and stepped back, while both Andy and Rob held their guns ready for business. Tubby watching saw that the former continued to keep his eyes fastened on the chimney of the low bunk-house all the while he talked; and from that he drew conclusions.

"You're thinking, I expect, Rob," Tubby ventured to say, "that what goes up in the air must come down again; and that as the cat dropped into the wide-throated chimney he's just got to climb up again, sooner or later. Am I right, Rob?"

"A good guess, Tubby, believe me," chuckled Andy. "What we want to do now is to respectfully but firmly influence that unwelcome guest to get busy, and vamoose the ranch in a hurry. Say, I'm ready to give him the warmest kind of a reception as soon as he shows the tip of his whiskered nose above the top of the chimney."

"Here, Tubby, lend me a hand," said Rob, "and we'll try to coax Mr. Cat to vacate his present quarters. Andy, I'll lay my gun down alongside you here, and if yours isn't enough to finish the rogue, snatch up mine in a hurry."

Andy agreed to that, and so the other two walked forward again to the front of the long log building, where the door was situated. Tubby was curious to know how his companion expected to work that "influence" he spoke of, and cause the ferocious intruder to depart as he came. He awaited the outcome with considerable interest.

"First," said Rob, as though he already had his mind settled, "we'll pick up a few handfuls of these chips and twigs that are so plentiful."

"Whee! but burning the old cabin down to get rid of a cat that stays inside would be what they'd call heroic treatment, wouldn't it, Rob?"

"I'm not doing anything as severe as that, Tubby," said the other. "We're going to try the smoke cure. All animals are in deadly fear of fire, and smoke will cause even a horse to become fairly wild. We can make our little fire close to the door, and the breeze which happens to be just right, will carry some of the smoke under it, for notice that wide crack there. When the cat sniffs that odor you'll see how fast he scrambles up that chimney again."

It all looked very simple to Tubby now; so those Spanish courtiers who had been declaring that discovering America was no great task after Columbus had shown them how to stand an egg on an end, doubtless sneered and said it was easy enough.

The little heap of trash was ignited, and just as Rob had said, it began to emit a pungent smoke that was driven against and under the door by the breeze.

"Keep ready, Andy!" Rob called out. "I thought I heard a scratching sound just then!"

Tubby ran back so as to be able to see the crown of the low chimney. He was only in time, and no more, for even as he managed to glimpse the apex of the slab-and-hard-mud vent something suddenly came into view. As Tubby stared with round eyes he saw a monstrous wildcat crouching there, looking this way and that, as if tempted to give battle to its human enemies, by whom it had been dispossessed from the scene of its royal feast.

Then there came a loud crash. Andy had fired his gun. Tubby shivered as he saw the big feline give a wild leap upward and then come struggling down the slight slope of the roof, clawing furiously, and uttering screams of expiring fury.

Andy was ready to send in a second shot if it chanced to be needed, but this proved not to be the case, for the struggles of the stricken beast quickly ended. The three boys hurried forward, and stood over the victim of Andy's clever marksmanship. The cat was one of the largest Rob had ever run across, and even in death looked so terrible that Tubby had an odd shiver run through his system as he stared in mingled awe and curiosity down at the creature.

"Too bad in one way that the poor old thing couldn't finish his feast in peace," Tubby was saying, "but then I suppose it's the chances of war. There's always a state of open war between these bobcats and all men who walk in the woods."

"Well, I should say yes!" cried Andy, patting himself proudly on the chest. "I'll always call this one of the best day's jobs I ever did. Think of the pretty partridges, the innocent squirrels, the bounding jack-rabbits and such things, that I've saved the lives of with that one grand shot. If this beast lived three years longer it'd surprise you, Tubby, to count up the immense amount of game that it'd devour in that time. I never spare a cat under any circumstances."

"Do you think it was all alone in the cabin?" asked the timid one.

"We'll soon find out," Andy told him, as he saw to it that his gun was in condition again for immediate use, and then started toward the closed door.

Cautiously this was opened a trifle, and one by one the boys peered through the crevice; all agreed that there was nothing stirring, and so eventually they made bold to pass inside.

It was discovered that the uninvited guest had made free with some of the stores of the party, but after all, the damage did not amount to a great deal, possibly owing to the coming of Rob and his two chums on the scene shortly after the cat started chewing at the half of a ham it had dragged down from a rafter.

The boys quickly removed all signs of feline presence. Andy declared that he intended skinning his prize, for the pelt if properly cured would make quite an attractive mat for his den at home. It would be pleasant of a winter evening, when resting in his easy chair, to gaze down upon the trophy, and once again picture that stirring scene up there in Maine, under the whispering pines, hemlocks and birches.

They adjusted themselves to the new conditions with that free and easy spirit so natural in most boys. It was next in order to pick out the bunks they meant to occupy while in the logging camp; for there were signs to tell them which had been already chosen by Uncle George and his two guides; and of course, no one thought to settle upon any of these particular sleeping-places.

They soon had a fire burning, and the interior looked quite cheerful. Sitting there Tubby could easily picture what a stirring scene it must have been in those times long gone by when a dozen, perhaps even a score, of muscular lumber jacks lounged about that same dormitory and living room, waiting for the cook's call to supper.

Later on Tubby came up to Rob while the other was arranging some of the contents of his pack, "scrambled" more or less, as he called it, by being carried for several days on his back, and thrown about "every which-way."

"Look here, Rob," the fat scout said, "I happened to run across Uncle George's fresh log of the trip. He always keeps one, and I've even had the pleasure of reading about some exciting adventures he's met with in former years. So that's my only excuse for glancing at what he's jotted down here. The last entry is where he made up his mind to go over to the Tucker Pond to try again for that giant moose. And by the way, Rob, I was wondering whether our excited visitor of last night could be this big chap Uncle George is so wild to get?"

"Now that might be so," admitted the scout leader, "though

the thought hadn't occurred to me before. He certainly was a buster of a beast, though he went off so fast none of us more than got a glimpse of his size. Anything of unusual importance in the beginning of your uncle's log, Tubby?"

"Oh, he got a deer on the opening day of the season, and we'll probably find some of the venison around, if we look again sharply. Something did happen it seems, something that gave my uncle considerable unhappiness, too. He lost one of his two guides."

"What! did the man die here?" ejaculated the astounded Rob.

"Oh! my stars! no, Rob, not quite so bad as that," Tubby hastened to add. "He had to discharge the man because of something he'd done. Uncle doesn't say what it was, but he was both indignant and pained; because he thought a heap of Zeb Crooks, who had been with him many seasons. The man was stubborn, too, and wouldn't ask Uncle George to forgive him, or it might have all been patched up. So he sent him flying, and started off to Tucker's Pond with his other guide, a Penobscot Indian named Sebattis."

"Well, that's interesting, Tubby," remarked Rob. "It doesn't mean anything to us, though I can understand how sorry your uncle must have been to part with a man he used to consider faithful. So it goes, and lots of things happen that are disagreeable. I suppose he'll have just as good a time with the one guide to wait on him as when there were a pair."

Apparently Uncle George's troubles did not bother Rob to any extent; but there were things weighing on his mind though, during that afternoon, and these had a connection with the flight of that man in the aeroplane, over across the Canadian boundary line.

CHAPTER VIII
TUBBY HAS AN ADVENTURE

Tubby was particularly interested in looking around. He had heard so much about these hunting camps of his sport-loving relative that now he had the chance to see for himself he kept prowling about. It was Tubby who presently discovered a haunch of fresh venison. Andy immediately announced that the keen-nosed wildcat was not in the same class with the stout chum.

"Say, we can have a mess of *real* venison for our camp supper to-night," added the delighted Tubby. "Haven't we a warrant for taking liberties in that Notice, where Uncle George invites the pilgrim to enter, wait, and make merry? How can any one be merry without a feast? I'll take all the responsibility on my shoulders, boys, so make up your minds the main dish to-night will be deer meat."

Later in the afternoon Tubby wandered outside to look around.

"Don't go too far away and get lost, Tubby!" called out Rob, who himself was busily engaged.

"Oh, I don't mean to more than stretch my legs," came the reply. "Here's a bucket, and there must be a spring somewhere handy. I think I'd like a drink of fresh water. I might as well fetch some back with me. Yes, now I can see a beaten path leading from the door in this direction. Rob, I won't be gone long."

"All right, Tubby," Andy called out in turn. "If you don't turn up inside of half an hour we'll send out a relief corps to look for you. Be sure to fetch a supply of that spring water back with you. I'm getting a bit dry myself."

So Tubby walked off. He was feeling in the best of spirits. He believed his troubles were mostly in the past, and the immediate future looked as rosy as the sky at dawn. In another day or two Uncle George would surely turn up, when the little operation of having that paper signed could be carried out. Then for a week of unalloyed happiness, roving the pine woods, feasting on royal game, and enjoying the society of the world-wide sportsman at evening time, when sitting in front of a cheery blaze inside that bunk-house the boys would be entertained with wonderful stories of the amazing scenes Uncle George had run across during his long and adventurous career.

Tubby had no difficulty in following that beaten path. In going to and from the spring the guides had made such a plain track that even a worse greenhorn than Tubby might have kept right. In fact, to stray would have been unpardonable sin in the eyes of a scout.

It proved to be much longer than he had expected. Tubby fancied that there was another water place closer to the camp, though Uncle George for some reason of his own preferred this spring. The path turned this way and that, passing around high barriers of lopped-off branches, now dead, and beginning to decay as time passed. Tubby could not but shudder as he contemplated the effect of a stray lighted match thrown into one of these heaps of dead stuff, that would prove as so much tinder. He hoped they would not have the ill luck to witness a forest fire.

Finally he came to the spring. It was a fine one, too, clear and bubbling. Tubby lay as flat as he could, and managed after considerable exertion to get a satisfying drink of that cold water.

"My, but that is good!" he told himself, after he had once more resumed an upright position. "I don't wonder at them coming all this distance to get a supply of water. Now to fill my bucket, and trot back over the trail; and by the same token it won't be just as easy a job as coming out was. But then the boys will thank me for my trouble, and that's quite enough."

As Tubby started off, carrying the pail of water, he suddenly bethought himself once again of that tremendous bobcat Andy had killed. It occurred to Tubby that he had been informed such creatures were always to be found in pairs. What if the mate to the defunct cat should bar his way, and attack him, recognizing in him one of the party that had been the means of making her a feline widow?

Tubby did not like the idea at all. He cast numerous nervous looks about him, as he hastened his steps a little. As a rule he swept the lower branches of the trees with those keen glances, for if the bobcat were lying in wait to waylay him it would select some such roost for its hiding place.

Then all at once Tubby plainly heard a sound behind him, that was exactly like the swift patter of feet in the dead leaves and pine needles. He whirled around and immediately experienced one of the greatest shocks of his whole life!

In and out of the aisles of the forest a moving object came pattering along. Tubby saw that it was about knee high and of a singular dun color. To his eyes it looked terribly fierce!

"Oh, murder! It must be a savage wolf, come across from Canada!" was what he told himself, remembering something he had heard a man say while they were waiting at a little wayside station in Maine, about such beasts of prey having been unusually plentiful up in Canada in the preceding spring, and bolder than ever known before.

Tubby wanted to drop his water pail and run like mad. He also would have liked to give a series of shouts, not that he was frightened, of course, but to sort of alarm the animal and cause him to turn tail; but his tongue seemed to be sticking to the roof of his mouth in the queerest way ever, and which for the life of him he could not understand.

But while he still held on to the bucket Tubby did manage to get his legs in motion once more; he was far from being paralyzed. The animal kept advancing and stopping by turns. Tubby thought the wolf was laying a plan to surround him, when the beast trotted to one side or the other. Yes, and the cunning of the animal to wag his tail that way, and act as though pleased to see him! Tubby thought of that ancient fairy story about Little Red Riding Hood, and how she met a wolf on the way to her grandmother's home. They always were tricky creatures, no matter in what country found; but Tubby was on his guard.

By now at least he had managed to regain his voice, and when the wolf trotted closer than he thought was safe he would make violent gestures with his arms, and try to shoo him away. Apparently the beast did not know just how to catch

Tubby napping, for he continued to trot along, forcing himself to look as amiable, Tubby saw, as he possibly could, although not deceiving the boy in the least.

"You can't fool me with your making out to want to be friendly, you miserable old scamp!" he chattered, after he had actually put down the now only half filled bucket, the better to throw up both arms, and pretend to be picking up stones, all of which hostile actions caused the obstinate creature to dart away a short distance although quickly coming on again. "Get out, I tell you! Oh, why didn't I think to get the loan of Rob's gun! What if he tumbles me down in spite of all my fighting like mad! But, thank goodness, there's the cabin, and maybe I can make it yet!"

He did in the end, and burst upon the other pair like a thunderbolt, so that both boys scrambled to their feet, and Rob exclaimed:

"What ails you, Tubby? Have you seen that big bull moose again—and did he attack you?"

"Oh, Rob! Andy! The wolf! The wolf!" stammered Tubby, now completely out of breath; but he had said quite enough, for the two boys snatched up their firearms and darted out of the cabin.

Tubby waited, fully expecting to hear shots, and perhaps wild yelping. Instead he soon caught the sound of whistling, and then he heard the boys laughing heartily. While Tubby stared and waited they came back into the bunk-house. The panting fat boy was startled to see trotting alongside, leaping up again and again, his terrible "wolf"!

"W-w-what's all this mean, fellows?" he stammered in bewilderment, at the same time dimly comprehending how his fears had magnified the evil.

"Only that your wolf turns out to be a poor dog that's probably got lost in the woods and was trying to make friends with you," laughed Rob.

Tubby quickly recovered, and joined in the laugh. The joke was on him. He no longer declined to make up with the four-footed stranger. His heart was tender, and he repented having called the wretched beast so many hard names. Tubby was really the first to discover that the dog acted as though almost famished, sniffing around, and looking longingly up toward the hams that hung from the rafter.

"Oh, you poor fellow!" said Tubby. "I bet you're as hungry as can be. Haven't had a single bite for a whole day? I guess I know what that means. I'll fix you out in a jiffy, see if I don't; Uncle George will say I'm doing the decent thing by you, too. Here, Wolf, for I'm going to call you that just for a joke, watch me get you a hunk of the poorest part of that haunch of venison."

Tubby was as good as his word, too. The stray dog had reason to rejoice over the freak of fortune that had sent him in the way of these new friends. Indeed, he gave promise of turning out to be quite a welcome addition to the party, for all of the scouts were fond of pet animals that could show affection. Wolf duly licked Tubby's plump hand after being fed, as his only way of displaying dog gratitude.

So the long afternoon wasted away. As evening approached the boys gave up all hope of seeing Uncle George that day. But then none of them worried, for things had turned out splendidly so far, and they could find reason to hope for the return of the party within forty-eight hours at most.

Tubby was as good as his word, too, and cut off quite a bountiful supply of that nice fresh venison, which he cooked with some strips of bacon; for all of them knew that this was the only proper way in which such meat should be used, since it was too dry to be attractive otherwise.

They pronounced the supper "gilt-edged," which in boyish language means the acme of perfection. As every one, including even "Wolf," whose appetite seemed boundless, proved to be exceedingly hungry, the repast was a royal feast. Then they sat around the fire, chatting and telling stories. Tubby even started up one of their school songs, and being joined by the other pair, the low rafters of that bunk-house resounded with the glorious refrain. In days past sounds far less innocent, ribald language and loud oaths, may have been heard within those walls, for as a rule the sturdy lumber jacks are the roughest kind of men, as hard as some of the knots they strike with their axes.

An hour or so later the boys settled down for a good sleep. Wolf had been let out for a run, and did not come back again, so Rob said he must be feeling so refreshed after his feed that he wanted to take a turn around, possibly in hopes of finding his lost home; or again it might be he was desirous of running a deer, for Wolf was a guide's dog, they had determined.

When they all retired the dog had not shown up again. Andy said he was an ungrateful cur, deserting his friends in that fashion; but Tubby stood up manfully for the dog, declaring that it was only right he should want to find his own people.

The fire had been allowed to die down, and Rob meant to let it go out. To shut the glow from their eyes he had made use of a rude screen doubtless intended for this very purpose by Uncle George.

An hour, perhaps several, passed away. Then Rob felt some one clawing at his arm, after which a low whisper sounded close to his ear. It was Andy, and he had something to communicate that was quite enough to cause a thrill to shoot through the heart of the aroused scout master.

"Listen, Rob, and keep very still," said Andy softly. "There's some one outside the door trying to get in. I heard him try the latch and give a push; and I think he's gone to prowling around, trying each of the wooden shutters over the windows in turn."

CHAPTER IX
THE MAN OUTSIDE

"Sure you weren't dreaming, Andy?" whispered Rob, in turn, as, having listened for a brief time, he failed to catch any unusual sound.

"Not a bit of it," the other assured him. "I sat up and made certain of it before crawling out of my bunk. I tell you there *is* somebody outside there, and he's doing his best to get in, too."

The night wind was sighing through the pinetops, Rob noticed. Could Andy's imagination, excited by some dream, have conceived the idea that a would-be intruder was "fiddling" at the door, and endeavoring to find ingress? Rob was still undecided, but at the same time he considered it the part of wisdom to get out of his bunk and slip his feet into a pair of warm moccasins he always carried with him.

It was almost dark inside the long bunk cabin. The fire had died down, and even if there were still smouldering embers present the wooden screen hid them from sight.

Rob now became aware of the fact that Andy clutched something in his hands. The touch of cold metal told him it was a gun. This would indicate that the other fully believed what he asserted, and that some strange man was even then about to force an entrance into the cabin, possibly under the belief that no one was occupying the building at the time.

"There, did you hear that?" came again from the aroused Andy. "He's trying one of the window shutters. Rob, I remember that several of them are kind of loose. When he strikes one of those he can get it open easily enough, and then what's to hinder him pushing in the sash?"

"Well, there is something moving around out there, I do believe," muttered Rob.

"Oh, I wonder if it could be Wolf come back!" said an awed voice close to them.

"Hello! Are you there, Tubby?" questioned Rob cautiously, for neither of them had noticed that they were crouching close to the bunk selected by the third member of the party. Tubby, chancing to awaken, must have heard them whispering.

"Yes, but could it be the dog, do you think, Rob?" asked the fat scout eagerly.

"That's silly talk, Tubby," Andy told him, so softly that his voice would not have carried any distance, and might never have been distinguished from that crooning night breeze that rustled the hemlocks and passed gently through the pinetops.

"Dogs couldn't reach up and shake a shutter that stood five feet from the ground. It's a man, that's what; and we'd better figure on how we're going to give him the surprise of his life, if he gets inside here."

"Wait till I get my little hand electric torch," said Rob, who often carried one of these useful articles about with him; indeed, any fellow who has handled such a neat little contraption in an emergency knows that they are worth their weight in silver every time.

The one Rob had was very diminutive; in fact, a "vest-pocket edition," it was called; but upon pressing the button quite a strong ray would be thrown forward. He kept it handy when sleeping in the open.

"Tubby, get out of your bunk, and be ready to lend a hand," ordered Rob. The one addressed hastened to do as he was told.

"Tell me what I'm to do, Rob," he pleaded.

"Bring both your heads closer this way," continued the leader. "Now, this is the scheme: Tubby, you creep over to the fire, and when you hear me call out throw that wooden screen down, and then as quick as you can get a handful of the fine tinder on the fire, so as to set up a blaze. Understand?"

Tubby said he did, and accordingly Rob went on further:

"Andy and myself will try to find out which window the man is going to creep through, and we'll form a reception committee. When I turn on the light, you, Andy, be sure to cover him with your gun, ready to shoot if he attacks us. Get that, do you?"

On his part Andy assured the chief that he understood perfectly.

"Well, then," concluded Rob, "all I want to say is that after Tubby sees the fire begin to pick up he is to dart over and get my gun here, with which he, too, will proceed to cover the intruder. That's all. Now get busy, boys. Andy, come with me, and be careful not to strike your gun against anything so as to alarm him. Tubby, head over to the fireplace, and be ready to act!"

It was intensely exciting, Tubby thought, as he managed to cross to the end of the long bunk-house, where the yawning fireplace stood—the same gaping aperture down which that bobcat had dropped, and up which he had also climbed with such fatal alacrity later on, when dispossessed by reason of the acrid smoke fumigation.

Reaching the place assigned to him, Tubby felt of the wooden screen. He found that it would only require a smart push to send it flat, after which he could turn his attention to snatching up some of the fine dry tinder which had been arranged in a little pile close by; and as Tubby had paid more attention to the cooking than any one else, he ought to know to a dot where to find this "fire-starter."

Meanwhile, Rob and Andy had started to creep along close to the side of the log cabin wall. Rob was heading directly toward the spot where he had distinctly heard the last suspicious sound. If the prowler without had found that shutter fast he would just as likely as not examine the next one, and keep trying until he ran upon a damaged wooden cover which the winds had banged back and forth until it could no longer do full duty.

Yes, there was some one shaking the next shutter which had been used to keep the drifting snow out when the loggers were in camp during the long winter months. As the two boys crept closer they could hear a grumbling sound, just such as might proceed from a disappointed man who was being continually baffled in his efforts to force an entrance.

Rob had been thinking as he moved, and several possibilities had in turn taken possession of his active mind. Could this be

Uncle George himself, come back to the abandoned logging camp, and who upon finding the door barred from within, was now trying to gain an entrance? At first Rob rather favored this idea, but he quickly realized how slender a hold it had in the way of plausible facts.

In the first place the sportsman would hardly come back minus his Indian guide, unless Sebattis, too, had proven false, and had to be sent flying like Zeb Crooks. Then, again, if he suspected that some passing hunters were occupying the bunk-house, having accepted the invitation to enter and make themselves at home, why should not Uncle George call out and ask them to open the door to him? No, there was something much more suggestive and suspicious about this event than the return of the mighty Nimrod. This unknown party did not suspect that the cabin was occupied; he meant to get in, perhaps to make free with the property left there by Uncle George.

In a word, Rob was more than half convinced already that he knew who the man outside, fumbling with the various wooden shutters, must be—no other than that same Zeb Crooks, who possibly had come sneaking back, knowing the intention of his former employer to leave the camp unprotected for a few days—come back to rob the place of anything valuable that he could find and sequester.

Rob did not bother trying to communicate this to Andy, for there was no need, and it would hardly have been politic, with the man outside so close to them. He was now at the next window, and Rob believed that the crisis was at hand, for the man gave a satisfied grunt as though things were finally working to suit his purposes.

So he nudged Andy, as if to warn him to be on the alert, though truth to tell there was little need of this, for the other scout was fully aroused every second of the time, with his gun clutched in nervous hands ready to do his duty when the call came.

Yes, the window was being shoved back now, and the man still muttered to himself. One thing sure, he never dreamed that the cabin had occupants, though how the door came to be fastened on the inside must have puzzled him somewhat.

The eyes of the boys had become so used to the semi-darkness that they were able to fairly make out the window, once the shutter had been drawn back. They could also see some sort of movement there. Having given the swinging sash a push that sent it inward, the man was now thrusting his head and shoulders through the small opening.

Rob knew the difficulties attending such an awkward entrance. He felt almost certain that the party, even if not clumsy in his movements, would likely tumble to the puncheon floor when he finally gave the last push. That was the very moment Rob figured on springing his surprise. The man would be caught unawares, and least able to defend himself or spring at them.

When he heard a scuffling sound, and saw the window no longer obstructed by a dark form, Rob knew the crisis was upon them.

CHAPTER X
NEATLY DONE

As the scout master suddenly pressed the button of his little hand torch and threw the expanding ray of light straight ahead, he called out in a loud voice:

"Go to it, Tubby, Andy!"

There was a loud crash. Tubby had obediently thrown the wooden fire screen over to the floor, and was trying to snatch up some of the fine tinder that would burst into a brilliant flame almost as soon as it reached the still hot embers on the hearth.

Andy, too, was equal to the emergency, and had his gun leveled directly at the figure of the sprawling man. There was a grim suggestiveness about the way in which all these things worked that must have staggered any one thus taken completely by surprise.

"Lie just where you are, unless you want to get hurt!" cried Rob, in an authoritative voice. "If you make any attempt to get up, or show fight, you'll have to take the consequences, and they'll not be pleasant, either. Understand that, Zeb Crooks?"

"Oh, that's who it is, eh?" burst from Andy. Tubby too must have seen a sudden light, though he was really a busy boy and did not bother to express his astonishment; for no sooner had he seen those fine bits of dry resinous wood begin to flash up than, remembering his instructions, he waddled across the floor, much after the fashion of a fat duck, and, securing Rob's gun, hastened to join the group near by.

Already the resuscitated fire had begun to illuminate the interior of the bunk-house. The glow disclosed a most singular scene, and one the boys would often remember with a smile.

The big man on the floor was staring at the trio of lads with a strange mixture of emotions depicted on his swarthy and bearded face. Evidently he was sorely puzzled to account for their presence there, when he had firmly believed the building to be wholly without occupants. He may have struck a match and read the "Notice" which the boys had not removed from the outside of the door.

"Who might the lot of you be?" he asked, still squatted there as he had fallen after forcing his entrance, with his rifle alongside, though he dared make no move toward regaining possession of the weapon with those two guns wavering back and forth so close to his face.

Rob bent over and quietly secured possession of the repeating rifle. The action showed him to be a diplomat of the first water, for in so doing he cut the claws of the wild beast they had trapped.

"We'll talk with you after we've made sure you're not going to give us any trouble, Zeb. Tubby, step over and fetch the piece of rope that's hanging from the peg yonder."

Tubby obeyed with alacrity—for him. Rob, taking the gun from his hands, gave another order.

"My friend, please accommodate us by rolling over on your face, and holding both your hands behind you. We mean to tie them there, wrist to wrist. It'll do no good for you to grumble, because it's just got to be done."

The intruder was a strong and bronzed fellow, who might easily have held two of the scouts out from him could he have gotten his hands on them; but then a boy in possession of a gun is as much to be respected as though he measured up to the full stature of manhood, and evidently the fellow appreciated this fact.

Still he did look disgusted as he proceeded with rather ill grace to do as Rob had ordered. It was almost comical to see his huge figure sprawled out there on the floor, with fat Tubby seated on his legs, and endeavoring to do a neat job with the rope-end. Rob was watching to make sure that there was no bungling; he did not believe in poor workmanship.

"Cross his hands so, Tubby, with the wrists together," he directed. "Now begin to wrap the rope around—draw it fairly tight. We don't want him getting loose on us, you understand.

When Uncle George comes back from the Tucker Pond he'll know what he wants to do with a thief!"

There was a loud growl from the man whose face rested sideways against the floor.

"Hold on, thar, kid," he said savagely, "you don't want to be so free applying such langwidge as that, 'ca'se it cuts to the bone. I may have been a fool to turn on Mr. Hopkins, and act stubborn-like, but I'm no thief! Mebbe onct in a while in times gone by I've shot deer out o' season, and busted the game laws, but I never in my life did take anything as belonged to anybody else, never, so help me."

Rob did not say anything until Tubby had finally completed his job, puffing over it as though the effort required every atom of breath he could command.

"Now, Tubby, help me get him over here, where he can rest against the wall," Rob said. "I know it's going to be mighty uncomfortable for him, fastened up this way, but nobody's to blame but himself."

"Huh, guess that's correct, younker!" grunted the man. "I sartin sure did make a fool o' myself, and I oughtn't to grumble if I have to pay up for it. But I'm plumb up against it now, seems like."

"Then you are Zeb Crooks?" asked Rob.

"Yep, that's who I am," came the unhesitating reply.

"Mr. Hopkins, who is the uncle of this boy here, discharged you only a day or two ago, didn't he?" continued the scout master, watching the play of emotions on the swarthy face of the Maine guide and trying to read what lay back of them.

"Waal, we had a little misunderstanding, you might say, and I was sorter set in my way. Mr. Hopkins, he seen there wouldn't be no sense o' us tryin' to pull together, so he up and paid me a hull month's wages and told me my room was a heap sight more agreeable to him than my company. I was that mad I jest up and cleared out o' the camp, and started across kentry toward my home, which is away back nigh Moosehead Lake."

"But it seems you changed your mind some, and turned back," remarked Rob drily.

"Jest what I did, younker," admitted Zeb contritely.

"You had a reason in doing that, of course?" continued the boy.

"Well, I guess so!" chuckled Andy scornfully, as though he considered that a superfluous question when they had caught the discharged guide creeping into the bunk-house and evidently meaning to purloin the best of the stores left there by the hunting party.

"Keep still, Andy," Rob hastily snapped, for he knew the other did not look as deeply into things as he ought, but often judged them in a superficial way.

Zeb glared at Andy as though he could give a pretty good guess what the other had in mind. The guide did not feel as kindly toward Rob's thin companion as might be the case with regard to the scout leader himself.

"My reason was jest this," he said firmly: "the more I got to thinkin' about how good Mr. Hopkins had been to me and my fambly for the ten years he's been hiring me as his head guide up here, an' over in Canada, why, the more I felt ashamed o' what I'd said an' done. The stubborn feelin' died away, an' I was plumb sorry. I jest stopped short on the way to Wallace, an' camped, so I could think it over some. An' there I stayed two days, a-wrestlin' with the nasty streak that had got aholt o' me. Then I guess I come to my senses, for I made up my mind I'd tramp back here and eat humble pie. Once I'd got to that point, nothin' couldn't hold me in, an' so I kim along. When I struck a match an' read that 'ere notice on the door, I figgered that Mr. Hopkins ought to be back in a day or so, an' that I made up my mind I'd wait here for him. Then I couldn't understand why the door was fast, but I remembered thar was a loose shutter, an'—well, I kim in."

Rob wondered whether the guide were telling the truth. He more than half believed that it was a straight story, for the man looked penitent enough, and was surely humiliating himself to thus acknowledge his faults before boys who were strangers to him.

"Huh! Do you believe that yarn, Rob?" asked Andy, who it may as well be admitted was rather skeptical by nature, and apt to think the worst of any one whom he suspected not to be on the level.

"I don't know what to think," said Rob hastily. "It may be just as Zeb tells us, but he will admit himself that his actions looked mighty suspicious, and also agree that we are perfectly justified in keeping him tied up until Tubby's uncle comes. Safety first is often a good motto for scouts to follow."

"Oh, that's all right, boys!" sang out the big guide, as cheerfully as a man who faced a long and tiresome period of captivity might be expected to appear. "'Course you couldn't expect to take my simple word for it. None o' you knows me. Mr. Hopkins, he's slept alongside o' me for ten years. I ain't afraid o' what he'll say when he comes back from Tucker Pond. Do jest as you think best. I'm goin' to take my medicine—and grin. I deserve the worst that could happen to me, arter treatin' my best friend like I done."

Rob liked the way in which he said this; it drew him closer to the man than anything else could have done. When any one has been foolish, and committed an indiscretion, repentance and frank admission of the wrong are after all the best signs of a return to reason.

"We'll make you as comfortable as we can for the night, Zeb," he told the guide. "In the morning we'll see what we can do about it."

"Jest as you say, sir; I guess I kin stand it. So you youngsters are Boy Scouts, be you? I got a nephew down at Waterville as belongs to the organization. When I was thar I thought his troop a right smart bunch o' kids. The stunts I showed 'em about things connected with the woods pleased the boys a heap. If I had a son, he'd have to jine the scouts, or I'd know the reason why, 'cause I believes in the things they stand for, every time, but my kids is all three gals."

"Well, he knows how to soft-soap, all right," muttered Andy, still suspicious.

Rob had a pretty firm conviction that Zeb Crooks belied his name, and that he was as straight as a die. Still, it would hardly do to be too hasty in freeing him; they had better wait until morning at least, when all of them had cooled down and the matter might be properly debated and settled, majority ruling as it generally did in such matters. Rob felt pretty certain that he would have the backing of gentle-hearted Tubby, in case he wished to remove Zeb's bonds.

Rob said nothing further, though he undoubtedly did a heap of thinking. With the assistance of his comrades he managed to get Zeb into one of the lower bunks. The man said he was fairly comfortable, and would doubtless manage to get some sleep, though his position was awkward, and of course his hands would feel "dead" from lack of circulation.

"I sure hopes you'll decide in the mornin' to believe me, boys, and undo these here cords," he remarked, with unction, as they turned to leave him.

"Perhaps we may; wait and see," Rob told him.

Andy shook his head and looked unhappy. Plainly he could not get it off his mind that the guide was what his name signified; and even though he had served Uncle George for ten years, doubtless he had been deceiving the good man all the time, only he had not been found out until now. Andy meant to "keep one eye open" during the remainder of the night, as he privately informed Tubby, thereupon causing that worthy further uneasiness.

They had thought to throw more fuel on the fire before climbing back into their bunks, so that the room would be lighted more or less during the rest of the night. If Andy chose to remain on guard, he was welcome to do so for all the others cared.

Tubby himself could not immediately get to sleep, for a wonder. Truth to tell, he was busy trying to figure out whether Zeb Crooks was a clever rascal or a blunt, honest backwoods guide, whose main faults possibly might lie in the possession of an easily aroused temper and a stubborn will.

Once or twice Tubby lifted himself on one elbow and stared hard toward the bunk where they had stowed the prisoner. He wondered if Andy could know better than Rob, and whether the big rough man right then might be working his hands free. Suppose Zeb should get loose, would he be tempted to turn the tables on them? Tubby tried to imagine how it would feel to have his wrists triced up like the legs of a fowl bound for the market. He did not believe he would fancy the sensation over well; and perhaps he should feel grateful to Andy because that worthy had promised to keep watch.

Then Tubby leaned forward and listened more carefully. Some one was sleeping soundly, that was sure, and the heavy breathing certainly came from the next bunk, where that alert guardian of their safety, Andy, had taken up his lodging. Tubby gave a scornful snort.

"Huh, a nice sentry he'd make, if our lives depended on his keeping awake! Guess I might as well drop off myself. If Zeb gets free while we sleep, and skips out, why, it's just as well."

After that all was still in the bunk-house. Even the man whose hands were so painfully fastened together must have made the best of a bad bargain and managed to get a certain amount of sleep; from which fact it would appear that Zeb's mind was perfectly at ease, now that he had decided to do the right thing.

The night passed away, and dawn came at length. It was about this time that all of them were awakened by certain noises without. At first they fancied that the hunting party must have returned and were beating at the door demanding admittance.

Then suddenly Tubby was observed "making a bee-line" for the door as fast as he could go. As Rob and Andy tumbled from their bunks they saw him fumbling with the bar, which he dropped before either of the others could call out. With that Tubby flung the door open, and in frisked an active object that seemed to want to fairly devour the stout chum. Tubby was crying:

"It's Wolf come back to us again, don't you see? Good boy, you didn't mean to desert your new friends, did you? Hey! Keep down there, and don't eat me alive, please."

CHAPTER XI
ZEB MAKES GOOD

Since they had been aroused, and the dawn was at hand, there was no use of going back to their blankets again. So the boys finished their simple dressing, and washed up outside the door. Tubby declared the air was as cold as the Arctic regions and it must surely be some degrees below freezing, two assertions that hardly bore out each other.

Zeb Crooks was gotten out of his bunk. Rob had made up his mind to release the other. He now believed the story the repentant guide had so frankly told them, and thought it would be too humiliating for Zeb to be found tied up by a trio of boys, when his employer returned.

But Rob took his time about carrying this out, though he had already obtained the backing of Tubby in the scheme. While the latter was preparing breakfast, and Andy had stepped out, gun in hand, for a little walk around, in hopes of seeing something in the line of game on which he could prove his skill as a marksman, the scout leader walked over to where the big guide sat with his back against the wall.

"You still say, do you, Zeb," he commenced, "that you meant to stay in the cabin here until Mr. Hopkins came back, and then ask him to overlook your foolishness?"

"I sartin did, youngster," affirmed the other vehemently, and then adding, "Thar was times when I got plumb skeered, because I hated to think of meetin' that look in my boss's eyes. I even considered whether I had ought to stay and take his money agin, arter I'd been so mean. I tried to write a leetle note I was calculatin' to leave here, in case my nerve give out and I slipped away again."

"A note do you say?" demanded Rob quickly. "Did you keep it, Zeb?"

"Shore I did, sir. It's right here in my pocket, tho' mebbe arter all I'd a-stayed the thing out, and then I needn't use it. But I didn't know, I wasn't right sartin I could stand for it."

Rob leaned over, and after fumbling around for a short time managed to find the well-thumbed paper. Evidently Zeb's education lay mostly in an extensive knowledge of woodcraft and the habits of wild animals, for he could not have spent much time learning to spell, or in applying the ordinary rules of grammar. Rob might have smiled at the primitive product of the big guide's untrained hand only for the fact that somehow his eyes were strangely blinded while he read.

"Mister hopkins, der sur, I ben the bigest fule livin' i gess to ack like i done with the best frend i ever had, and sur i wanted to tell you this but i dident hav the nerve to stay. i em agoin hum an wen i look in the cleer eyes of my gal Ruth as was named after yur own ded wife i feel like kickin myself, but i shore do hope yo kin forgiv Zeb Crooks and mebbe next year hire me agin. I had my leson, sur, thats rite, an never agin siz i. An i hopes yo git that big bull moose this time thats awl.

Zeb Crooks."

Rob folded that soiled sheet of paper, torn from a memorandum book. He meant to keep it, and on the sly show it to Mr. Hopkins, who could appreciate the manly nature that had thus conquered in the battle with an evil spirit. Andy would not appreciate such a message, for he must suspect that it was only intended to blind the eyes of a trusting person and conceal the man's real intentions. Yes, Tubby might see it, some time or other. Rob intended to keep it always.

"Well, Zeb," he went on to say cheerfully, to hide the emotion he felt, "we've concluded to set you free. You can stay around until they get back from the Tucker Pond, when there'll be a chance to fix matters up with Mr. Hopkins."

"I'm shore plumb pleased to hear that, younker," declared the guide, grinning. "It ain't none too pleasant to be tied up, and some humiliatin', seein' as how you are only boys. The sorest thing o' all would have been to let *him* see me this way."

"That's going to be all right, Zeb," said Rob, much impressed with the justice of this remark. "I'll see to it that none of us tell him we made you a prisoner. We believe what you've been telling us. In fact, I thought you were straight from the beginning, but that note clinched it for me."

He soon had the rope unfastened. Tubby, looking over from the fire, nodded his head in appreciation. Andy, coming in shortly afterward, failed to make any disagreeable remark, from which it might be judged that he had begun to think better of his former opinion with regard to Zeb's honesty.

The guide acted as though nothing out of the way had happened. He assisted Tubby in getting breakfast, just as he was in the habit of doing for his employer. Indeed, Zeb seemed to improve upon acquaintance, and Rob felt certain he had not made a mistake in tempering justice with mercy.

They had a merry time of it at breakfast. The boys were light-hearted by nature, and Zeb seemed to be growing to like them very much. He asked many questions in connection with their past experiences. They had any quantity of incidents to relate, some of which caused the Maine guide to open his eyes wide; for the accounts Tubby and Rob gave of what wonderful things they had seen when with the fighting armies in Belgium and France were enough to thrill any one to the core.

Later on that morning Andy started forth again, bent on picking up some game. He was advised by Rob to be careful and not get lost, an injunction which he promised to heed.

Rob had been more or less anxious during the night. He could not get it out of his mind that the man who piloted that aeroplane had been spying out the land on the other side of the border for some dark purpose. Rob had half fancied he heard a distant heavy sound that might be caused by an explosion, though on second thought he decided that he was wrong.

Two nights had passed without anything of this sort happening. He wished Mr. Hopkins would get back to the camp so he could consult with so experienced a man as Tubby's uncle must be, and decide what their duty should be.

Andy did not come back until after the others had started to eat lunch. When they saw the number of plump partridges he carried they congratulated him on his good luck. Rob had anticipated something of this sort, having heard a number of shots in rapid succession, so suspecting that the hunter had struck game.

"But, shucks!" Andy went on to say in a disgusted tone, "I'm almost ashamed to tell you how easy they came to me. Why, after I'd flushed the covey they went and alighted in a tree with wide-spreading branches. There half a dozen of the silly birds perched on a lower limb, and I picked off one as nice as you please. Still, to my surprise, the rest didn't fly away, but just sat there, craning their necks to look down and see what their companion was doing all that kicking and fluttering on the ground for. Guess the gumps thought it was a new sort of partridge cake-walk. Anyway I nailed the second one, then a third and a fourth, and, why, would you believe me, I actually got the fifth when the last bird flew away. It was too easy a job; like taking candy from the baby. Don't call me a hunter, I feel more like a butcher right now."

"But, Andy, they're nice and fat," cooed Tubby, running his hand admiringly down the speckled breast of one bird. "I'm figuring on rigging up a dandy spit so we can cook it in front of the fire. I've tasted chickens cooked that way at a restaurant in the city, and my! but they were delicious."

"They did use a spit ages and ages ago," laughed Rob, "which goes to show that after all our forefathers knew a good thing or two that hasn't been improved upon in all these centuries. Here's hoping you have the best of luck, Tubby. If you need any help, call on me."

Tubby did put in most of the afternoon on that job. Zeb took it upon himself to attend to the fowls, which he dressed most carefully. Tubby was more than glad that the little company had received an addition, for if there was one thing he disliked doing it was cleaning birds or fish.

Along in the late afternoon he had the right kind of a fire for his purpose. With all the birds fastened on his home-made spits, which could be revolved with a clock-like motion, Tubby set to work to prove himself a master *chef*. Indeed, as the work went on, and the revolving birds began to take on a brown hue the odors that permeated every part of the long bunk-house were enough to set any ordinary hungry boy half crazy. Andy was seen to hurriedly take his departure, after finding out from Tubby that supper would not be ready for at least half an hour; it looked as though he for one could not stand it to "be so near, and yet so far."

When Tubby grew tired or overheated he would give the willing Zeb a chance to make himself "useful as well as ornamental," as Tubby jokingly remarked. He and the big Maine guide were the best of friends. It looked as though Zeb would have a pretty good advocate with the uncle in case any were needed to straighten out his affairs with Mr. Hopkins.

Finally the summons was beaten on a skillet, always welcome to those who have been hanging around, and suffering cruel tortures because the minutes seem to drag with leaden feet. Every one pronounced Tubby's enterprise a most wonderful success. Partridges may have tasted fine before, when cooked in one of those hunters' earthen bake-ovens that resemble a fireless cooker so much; but in that case they would have simply been as though steamed, and lacked all that brown crispness.

Still no sign of the party from the Tucker Pond. They must surely come back by another day, Rob thought, with a feeling akin to uneasiness; for once more he dreaded what a night might bring forth, his thoughts being again carried across the line into the country whose sons were in the trenches over in Belgium and the North of France.

So Rob felt that his mind would be much relieved if only another day saw Mr. Hopkins, in order that he might shift the burden to older shoulders. Somehow it seemed to the anxious scout master as though some sort of responsibility had been placed upon them because they chanced to see that airman making his reconnoissance two days before.

The night was now upon them. Little did any of those three boys suspect what thrilling events were destined to take place in their lives and how their patriotism would be tested before another daybreak came. They sat around as usual, and made merry. Tubby played with the dog, for Wolf had not offered to run away again. It was concluded that he must have given up all hope of ever finding his former home; or else felt quite contented to remain with his new masters, who fed him so abundantly.

It was getting well along toward nine o'clock, and some of them had even commenced to show signs of being drowsy, for it must be remembered that they had not been allowed to enjoy a full night's sleep on the preceding night.

Andy said he would step outside and see what the signs promised in the heaven for the next day. He pretended to be quite a weather prophet. He had hardly closed the door behind him, it seemed to Tubby, than they heard him coming hastily back again. He seemed excited, too, a fact that caused Tubby to struggle to his feet, though the others were already ahead of him.

"I wish you would all come out here and listen," said Andy. "I may be mistaken, and, perhaps, after all, it's only some freak of the breeze whining through a hole in the cabin wall; but, honest to goodness, it struck me that it was some one calling in the distance, and calling for help, too."

CHAPTER XII
A SCOUT'S FIRST DUTY

"My stars! what's going to happen next, I wonder!" Tubby said half to himself, as they all made a rush for the outside, Andy leading the way, as became the first discoverer.

"Now, keep real quiet and listen!" cautioned Andy, after they had reached the open air.

Their hearts beat doubly fast, and knocked tumultuously against their prison walls. The boys fairly held their breath, such was their eagerness to hear, and learn whether Andy could have been mistaken.

A whole anxious minute crept past. To Tubby it seemed an eternity, for he was trying to do without breathing at all, a rather rash experiment for any one, and especially for a stout fellow of his build. Something came floating on the gentle night wind.

"There, didn't you all hear it?" cried Andy exultantly.

"We certainly did," said Rob instantly.

"Sounded a little like one of those winnowing whoop owls to me," ventured Tubby, but he was immediately squelched by the first discoverer.

"Owl nothing! Whoever heard an owl call out 'Help! Oh! Help!'?"

"I felt pretty sure it was that," replied the scout master. Turning to the experienced Maine woodsman he added: "How about that, Zeb, owl or a human cry for assistance?"

"I guess as how it wa'n't anything that carried feathers as called, sir," Zeb quickly answered. His backing Andy up made Tubby display further signs of uncommon excitement.

"Somebody is in serious trouble, boys," burst from Tubby's lips almost impulsively. "We've *got* to start out and help him, no matter who he is, or what's happened to him. That's scout logic, I take it—save me first, and scold me afterwards, as the

boy said when he was drowning and a man on the bank began
——"

"The rest will keep, Tubby," said Rob. "You'll have to stay
here, and keep the fire going for us. Three ought to be enough
for the job. Get the guns, Andy and Zeb. I'll take that lantern
belonging to Mr. Hopkins. We may need some light in the
woods. Be quick about it, everybody. There, he's calling
again. Perhaps I'd better answer him."

Rob sent out a loud *hallo* that could easily have been heard
half a mile away at any time. Without waiting to find out
whether the unknown made any reply, he shot into the
bunkhouse and started to apply a match to the ready lantern
which had been discovered during the day hanging from a peg
behind some extra garments.

Tubby did not look very happy. True, he would be saved from
quite a tramp, and that counted for something. He was not at
all tired, and would, had he been given the chance, much
prefer accompanying his mates. Still, Tubby was a good
scout, and had long ago learned the value of unquestioning
obedience to authority. Rob was above him in rank as the
leader of the Eagle Patrol, as well as acting scout master of
the Hampton Troop, and what he said in such a decisive
manner must go.

So Tubby determined that he would build the fire, and have
everything warm and comfortable against the return of his
chums. He could shut and bar the door; yet, and—Rob
evidently did not mean to take his gun along with him
(thinking two would be quite enough), so there would be that
to depend on, if any danger threatened.

It took the trio but a part of a minute to get ready, so eager
were they to be on the move. They hurried out of the door.
Tubby watched them depart, standing in the open doorway.
How weird the lantern did look bobbing along at the side of
Rob. Tubby wondered what sort of discovery they would
make. If some one was in trouble, could it be his uncle who,
on attempting to return to the logging camp alone, had fallen
and broken a limb? Or, on the other hand, had some
woodsman cut himself severely with his ax, and weak from
loss of blood, fallen on the road to the camp, able only to
weakly call for help?

No matter what it turned out the very thought of some one being in need of help thrilled honest Tubby, who would have "walked his legs off," as he often declared, to render assistance. Further the bobbing lantern went. The murmur of his chums' voices, too, died away in the distance. Suddenly he could no longer glimpse the light, and all was dark and mysterious beyond. Then only did Tubby deign to go in and close the door after him, being careful to make use of the handy bar that nested in the sockets on either side.

He built up a roaring fire, because somehow, the cheery crackle of the devouring flames felt like company to him. They had an abundant supply of good firewood, some of which Tubby had himself gathered from around the former lumber camp.

Tubby picked up Rob's gun and sat looking into the fire, doubtless seeing all sorts of queer pictures there, as boys sometimes will. Evidently his thoughts were on other things, for after a while he approached the exit, unfastened the bar, and opening the door a little stood there listening, oh! so eagerly.

That was a real owl crooning to his mate now in the big hemlock over the way, although at first Tubby thought it might be the same sound they had heard before. He wondered whether they had been "fooled," and if it would turn out to be a fool's errand that took his chums and Big Zeb forth on that mercy trip.

Tubby had to chuckle, proudly remembering that it had been himself who had suggested "owl," though Andy instantly made fun of him for so doing. The joke would be on Andy then, should it eventually turn out that way.

Hearing no further sound from those who had gone away, nor a repetition of the supposed cry for help, Tubby reluctantly closed the door, put the bar in place, and taking his seat again before the fire, resumed his vigil.

Meanwhile the three were making their way through the woods. The darkness was not intense, and possibly they could have gotten along quite well without the lantern. Nevertheless, none of them was sorry for having it; more than one stumble was spared them on account of it.

They had noted well the quarter from which the faint cries had come, and were now heading in that direction. All was still around them, save for the rustle of scurrying little feet in the dried pine needles, as perhaps a fox on the prowl for his supper slipped out of the way; or possibly it may have been a mink, for there was some sort of stream close by, which emptied into the river down which the logs had been sent when the big spring drive was on.

"We're heading right, don't you think, Zeb?" asked Rob presently, being desirous of confirming his own opinion, and knowing that the experienced guide and woodsman could be depended on to be accurate.

"Straight as a die, younker," the man told him, and then added: "I'm a heap s'prised to see how you boys kerry on. 'Tain't every lad from the towns that could pick out a sound like you done, and then direct that way. I guess thar must be a heap o' sense in this here scout business, an' I gotter take off my hat to it, that's a fack."

Words like that give a scout a warm feeling in the region of his heart. Appreciation is always welcome when genuine; to be complimented by an expert like Big Zeb, the man who had served Uncle George for ten years as guide and handy man in camp, was thrice pleasant. Still, both Rob and Andy were used to hearing people say nice things, and it never brought on a case of "swelled head" with such sensible fellows.

A short time later on Rob spoke again.

"I tried to take into consideration the fact that the wind wasn't altogether favorable, and also that the chap called as if he might be hoarse from weakness or excitement. So I figured that he couldn't be more than a quarter of a mile off at the time. How did you make out, Andy?"

"Oh! I thought he was further than that, say two-thirds of a mile as the crow flies; but I didn't count on his being exhausted, as you say, Rob."

"If you asked me, younkers," said Zeb, "I'd fix it atween the two o' you. I should say we'd a'ready gone nearly a quarter o' a mile from camp. But we ain't heard nary a sign o' him yet. S'pose we let out a call, and tried fur a raise?"

"A good idea, Zeb," admitted the scout master. Raising his voice he called out: "Hello! there, where are you?"

Almost immediately they heard a half-stifled cry that seemed to be full of partly suppressed joy.

"This way, over here to your left, man! Oh! please hurry up. I'm in a sair bad fix, and there's an awfu' need o' haste!"

The words thrilled them once more. Now they were sure that it was no imaginary summons that had lured them from the warm fire; someone *was* there in the depths of the pine woods, unable to help himself, strange as that might seem.

"Rob, that sounded more like a boy's voice than a man's heavy tones," suggested Andy.

"Just what I was thinking," said the observing scout master. "Do you know there seemed a little odd twist in his way of speaking that made me think of Scotch Jock back in Hampton. Whoever this chap turns out to be, mark my words, he's got Scotch blood in his veins."

"There he calls out again, you notice," exclaimed Andy presently, "and we're heading right, it seems. I reckon he sees the light of our lantern, though we can't yet get the first glimpse of him."

"But we will very soon now," Rob assured him. "The last hail was close by."

They were consumed with both curiosity and eagerness to be of assistance. Neither of them could more than guess at what they were going to see; and it may be admitted that not even wise Zeb came anyway near to hitting the mark.

He may have figured that some one had fallen and injured his leg or ankle; or another sort of accident—a tree falling on him; being cut through by a misstroke of a keen-edged ax; or having his gun go off, when drawing it muzzle forward through some dense brush—as greenhorns often do at peril of their lives; but if they guessed for an hour they would not have dreamed of the remarkable sight that met their gaze.

"There, I think I can just manage to see him, Rob—over by that clump of birches that have sprung up where a mother tree was cut down years ago. Lift your lantern a bit and look."

Rob hastened to comply, and immediately remarked:

"Yes, I do see something dark on the ground. It moves. See, that must be his arm waving to us! We'll be with you, my friend, in a jiffy now. It's all right. We'll soon have you in camp, safe and sound, whatever has happened to you!"

Rob was saying this out of the kindness of his heart. He realized that undoubtedly the other must have been in both physical and mental distress, or he would never have cried out as he had.

A minute later and they had drawn near enough for the strange truth to break upon them; and certainly it made both Andy and Rob stare as though they could hardly believe their eyes.

CHAPTER XIII
A THRILLING DISCOVERY

The light of Rob's lantern showed them a boy of about their own age. He was half on his knees, and seemed to be caught in some way so that he could not get away.

The light of Rob's lantern showed them a boy of about their
own age.

"Why, he's got his leg in a trap, don't you see, Rob?" gasped Andy, filled with horror at the very idea, for it seemed to portend the most serious consequences.

"It does look like an old rusty bear trap!" Rob admitted as they hurried on; Zeb instantly corroborated what he said by exclaiming:

"Jest what she are, an' no mistake. Jingo! I sartin sure hopes as how the boy ain't bad hurted. I've seen men that was lamed fur life arter being ketched by the jaws o' a bar trap. But this un seems old like, and mebbe the springs are weak."

All the same the unlucky victim of the trap had apparently not been able to free himself.

"I'm right glad ye've come!" called out the boy, showing a wonderful amount of nerve. "I shouted till I could hardly call above a whisper, and I was nearly crazy with fear that I'd have to stay here till mornin', when I heard you answer.

"Hurry, please, and get this old thing off me. Ye see I couldn't reach the second spring nohow, try as hard as I might. It hurt something fierce whenever I twisted around that way."

They were all bending down now. The first thing Rob noticed with a great feeling of relief, when he brought his lantern close to the prisoner of the rusty old bear trap, was that there were no signs of blood. This gave him fresh hope that the misfortune might not turn out to be quite so serious as he had at first anticipated; and also it proved that Zeb, a trapper of long experience himself, had hit the nail on the head when he said that the trap looked as if it might be old, and the springs weak in their action.

Apparently it had enough power to snap shut and hold fairly firm. Could the boy have borne heavily on both springs, he might have succeeded in effecting his release in the beginning.

Zeb immediately put his weight on the obstreperous spring. Andy pried back the unwilling jaws; whereupon Rob was able to take out the boy's leg from the trap.

The boy rubbed his hand tenderly up and down his leg at the point where it had been seized. He gritted his teeth, and winced a little, but quickly exclaimed as if in deepest gratitude:

"Hurts some, but the bone wasn't broken, and I'm unco' lucky. What's a black and blue bruise anyway? I can stand it, ye ken."

With Rob's help he managed to get on his feet, after which he immediately began to limp around, muttering to himself as he went, as though controlled by a mixture of emotions— thankfulness that it was no worse, gratitude because of the coming of these rescuers, and chagrin at having been caught in such a ridiculous situation.

Zeb meanwhile was examining the trap with the eye of an expert.

"Jest about worn out," he was saying, "an' she never'd hev held a bar in the wide world. Now, I wonder who put that no-good thing thar—no trapper as knowed his business, I'd say. Looks more like a kid's work than anything else."

"Yes, it was a boy," explained the late victim, "and the funny part of it all is that I should have happened on to the trap my cousin Archie told me he'd kept set for a month, over near the old logging camp."

"Archie was the lad's name, was it?" demanded Zeb quickly. "I remember that Cameron, the guide I used to pull with, and who came up this way last summer to settle, had a lad by that name."

"Well, Archie Cameron is my full cousin," explained the stranger. "I'm Donald McGuffey, ye ken, and I live over the line in a Canadian village. I'd been visitin' my relatives, and was on my way back home when this happened. Now I'm lame, and perhaps I can never get there in time to save them."

"What's that?" asked Rob suspiciously. "Are your folks in any danger? Did you get word that they were sick? Tell us what you mean, Donald, and if we can be of any further assistance to you we stand ready to do all we can, for we're scouts, you know, and it's our duty to hold out a helping hand every time."

"Oh! but that's fine of you!" cried the Canadian boy, shaking with emotion, which, of course, none of the others could as yet begin to understand. "Why, I'm a scout, too, though now I haven't got my uniform on. But, oh! I wonder if you would dare take it upon yourselves as comrades to stand by me through this terrible thing?"

"Terrible thing, what, Donald?" almost shouted the aroused Andy. "Speak up and let's know what it's all about. Why should we hesitate about helping you out? Who's going to hurt us for sticking to a comrade that's in distress?"

"Those awful men—they would be furious if they knew any one meant to interfere. Yes, they would even do muckle mair than tie ye up. I believe, in my bones, they are that wrapped up in their diabolical scheme they'd murder anyone who tried to break it up!"

"Speak plainer, Donald," snapped Rob. "We are wasting precious time while you throw out hints in that way. Tell us everything!"

The Canadian boy stopped limping around. He seemed to straighten up his figure, and they could now see that he was a tall and spare lad, as wiry as they make them over in the country beyond the border.

"It's just this, ye ken," he said earnestly. "They mean to blow up the bridge this verra nicht, in time to trap the regular munition freight that goes over at two in the mornin'!"

Rob and Andy exchanged horrified looks. Their worst fears were confirmed. Only for their having seen the evolutions of that spying aeroplane that crossed the line and hovered above the railroad embankment near where the trestle leading to the bridge lay, they might have been at a loss to comprehend what these startling words meant. But that much was very plain to them; in fact, as we have seen, Rob at least had been confident that the terrible plot had only been delayed, and not given up.

How had this Canadian boy learned of the truth? Plainly there was more for him to explain, though Rob could now understand the fearful mental suffering he must have endured, as well as the physical pain, on finding himself detained in that astounding fashion, when he was undoubtedly hastening as fast as he could go to carry his news to those guarding the threatened railroad.

"Come, tell us as quick as you can how you learned this, Donald," said Rob. "Two days ago we saw an aeroplane cross over, and we guessed then that perhaps the pilot was spying out the land, for there has been some talk of plotters here in the States in sympathy with Germany, who were trying to blow up munition plants in Canada, or doing something just as dreadful."

"Aweel, they've settled on destroying the long bridge across which so many loaded trains pass every twenty-four hours," said the other hurriedly, and with bated breath, owing to his increasing excitement. "I happened to overhear them talking while on my way to the river, after saying good-bye to my cousin, who was sick abed. I knew they were up to something, for I saw that they had a small German flag, which each one of them kissed as they sat around the fire. So I crept close up and listened, oh! with my heart nearly in my mouth. I soon learned that they were sure enough enemies of my country, and that they meant to strike a blow against the Allies before another morning, that for weeks and weeks would paralyze all traffic flowin' to the sea by this railway line."

"It was a brave act in your crawling up and listening," said the admiring Andy, as he laid a hand on the arm of the Canadian lad. "And make up your mind we're going to stand by you through thick and thin, Donald. Scouts should help each other, and that, you know, means just what it says."

"Go on and tell us the rest, please!" urged Rob.

"Why, after I had learned what they were scheming to do," continued the other promptly, greatly pleased at hearing those generous words spoken by impetuous Andy, "I knew I must get alang, if I wanted to be ahead o' the gillies. Ye ken I remembered hearing my cousin say he believed a Yankee sportsman and his guides would be over at the old logging camp; and sae I changed me course a bit, meanin' to drap in and see if they would nae helpit me carry the news across the line. Then, bad luck to it all, I had to deliberately step into the auld bear trap my cousin Archie had tawld me that he put out here a wheen o' time back."

"It was doubly unfortunate," said Rob, his voice full of sympathy.

"It made me verra mad, I assure ye," confessed Donald frankly. "Try as I would I could nae get me leg free, nor could I yet reach the spring to bear down on the same. I stood the pain the best I was able whenever I reached out, but it was a' no gude. And only for the luck o' ye hearing my shouts there I must ha' remained till the day came, and then it would ha' been far too late. But now I hae telled ye a' I must be on me way again, no matter how I hae to limp it."

"Hold on, Donald, not so fast," said Rob. "We are going with you!"

"Across the border, do you mean, Rob?" exclaimed Andy gleefully, for being of an adventurous spirit, nothing could have pleased him more than this.

"There seems to be no other way to foil those desperate conspirators. The Canadian authorities are none too friendly to us right now on account of numerous things that have happened and which they lay to German sympathizers crossing over secretly from our side. Yes, we must try to help our fellow scout do his duty to his country, which he loves just as much as we do our own native land."

"Oh, it makes my heart fairly jump to hear ye say that! It's braw lads ye air, baith o' ye, and I'll never forget it, never! My leg hurts, but I think it will get better after I use it a while. No matter how it pains me, I shall go on and on, even if I have to crawl and drag it after me, for I must carry the news to the guards. I would gie ten years o' life if only there was a way to flash it across the border to them richt now."

"First we must go back to the cabin," said Rob.

"Is it necessary, then?" asked Donald anxiously, as though fairly wild to be on his way.

"Yes, because there are several reasons," he was told. "We have a chum there who would never forgive us if we started on such a glorious expedition and left him behind. Then again, I have some salve that, rubbed on your leg, would do a lot of good and relieve the pain considerably. So let's start."

Donald may have had a good Scotch will of his own, but as he too was a scout, he had also learned to yield to those in authority. He seemed to guess intuitively that Rob *must* be a leader, perhaps from his positive way of saying things and possibly from Andy's deferring to his opinion.

They were soon hurrying along, Donald suppressing any groan as he continued to limp more or less.

"I hae not tauld ye all," he was saying. "I learned from what I heard them say while I hid in the bushes that they expected to set a mine under the trestle and connect it with a battery by a long wire. Then from a distance they could destroy the bridge just when the heavy freight train was passing over. Ye can understand what I suffered when I tell ye that my fayther is an engineer in the employ of that same railway and that he pulls the munition freight this verra nicht!"

CHAPTER XIV
ROB MAKES UP HIS MIND

"Whew, but that's doubly tough, I should say!" ejaculated Andy, when he heard this astounding declaration on the part of the boy whose cause they were about to champion.

Rob, too, was deeply concerned.

"Then it's easy to understand why you were so wild to get there in time to stop this horrible act," he told Donald. "It might be bad enough for the wretches to do something to cripple the railway services, so as to stop the flow of munitions; but it means a whole lot more to it when it's your own father whose life is placed in danger."

"Yes, and a fayther like mine, in the bargain," said Donald, so proudly that it was plain to be seen that the engineer was not without honor and love in his own family.

"If you hadn't thought that you possibly could get help here at the old logging camp," said Rob, "and cut across this way to see if the hunting party was still there, I suppose you'd have taken a different route?"

"Oh, ay," promptly answered the other.

"In that case you wouldn't have found yourself caught in that trap?" asked the leader of the Eagle Patrol, as the quartette hastened toward camp.

"I couldnae well be ketched in the auld bear trap set by me cousin Archie if it was half a mile awa' I ran, ye ken," Donald asserted naïvely.

"Well, we will be at the camp in a few minutes now," Rob went on to say, thinking to further encourage the poor chap, whom he knew to be suffering more mentally than he was physically. "Once we make it, we needn't be detained very long. I'm going to depend a whole lot on you to take us across the boundary by the shortest route possible."

"Ye can wager your last bawbee that I'm capable o' doin' it," came the reply, in such a tone of positive conviction that if

Rob had been entertaining any doubts on that score they were quickly put to rest.

"If you need any extra pilotin'," spoke up Big Zeb, "count on this chicken to do his best to kerry ye through."

"Then you mean to keep with us, do you, Zeb?" asked the scout master.

"I sartin do; that is, if ye want me along," the guide replied. "I'm an American born, and p'raps haven't had as much friendly feelin' for the Canucks 'cross the line as I might in times past, but, sir, when I hears how they are volunteerin' by the tens of thousands an' goin' away 'cross the ocean to fight 'ginst the Kaiser, I begins to change my idees consarnin' *that* brood. Now I thinks they air all to the good, an' I takes off my hat to them. Yes, an' arter hearin' what meanness this 'ere batch o' schemers is up to, I'd walk all the way to Labrador to upset their ugly game; that's me, Zeb Crooks, Maine woods guide."

"I'm glad to hear you say that, Zeb," said Rob heartily. "If you'd seen the terrible sights we did in Belgium and northern France, you'd feel that there was need for sympathy for those who are risking their lives to crush all military spirit and prevent a world war like this from ever happening again as long as men people the earth. That's what's taking these Canadian boys away from their homes, nearly four hundred thousand of them. It isn't alone that the empire they belong to is in danger, but the whole world is on fire, and the conflagration must be quenched. They believe it can be done only in one way, which is by winning this war. Of course, the Germans and their allies say it's just the opposite and that they are fighting for their very existence. Well, there's the camp!"

They could just glimpse delicate lances of light which managed to escape through the cracks or chinks between the logs that had not been fully filled afresh when the hunting party took possession of the bunk-house.

A minute afterward Andy was pounding at the door, but there was little necessity for this summons, because the listening scout within had heard the murmur of their voices and was already fumbling with the bar. So the friendly door was quickly flung wide open, and Donald found himself ushered into a warm and hospitable interior.

He and Tubby stared at each other, and with reason. Donald on his part may have thought that never before had he run across so fat a youth as Tubby Hopkins, who seemed to be fairly bursting his khaki clothes with plumpness. On his part, Tubby was naturally consumed with a burning curiosity concerning this young stranger—who he could be; what had happened to make him have such a perceptible limp; and, above all, why were Rob and Andy seeming to be in such a stupendous hurry?

"Sit right down here, Donald," said the scout master, indicating a rude bark chair close to the cheery blaze, "and I'll look up that magical salve. I know where I put it away in my pack. I give you my word you'll find it just the thing to soothe that bruised leg of yours. Andy, tell Tubby what's happened, and about our plan of campaign for invading Canada this very night."

"W-w-what?" gasped the other, his face the picture of both amazement and consternation.

"Oh, that's nothing, Tubby!" remarked Andy airily. "Now don't go to suspecting that we're meaning to do anything that's wrong. Just the other way, for the boot's on the other foot, since this is going to be an errand of mercy and meant to keep Uncle Sam from being accused of a grave breach of neutrality by the folks up in Ottawa."

"For pity's sake, what do you mean, Andy?" cried poor bewildered Tubby. "Please be good and explain it all in a jiffy. I'll certainly burst if you don't, I'm that keyed up now."

"I believe you will, sure enough, for I can hear the hoops of the tub creaking under the strain right now," chuckled the other; and then making a fresh start, he went on to say: "This is our jolly chum, Tubby Hopkins, Donald. We call him our Friar Tuck when we play at Robin Hood of the Greenwood Forest, you know. It is his uncle who has been hunting here and making his headquarters in this old logging camp, though just now he's up at the Tucker Pond trying for the big bull moose. Donald McGuffey, Tubby, a Canadian boy who belongs to the scouts in his town across the line and who's been visiting a cousin on our side."

Rob came hurrying up bearing a small zinc box such as salve is often kept in. He was down on his knees without asking questions and assisting the injured lad to roll up his trousers leg to the knee. It seemed that Donald had a wise and careful mother, for he was wearing, in addition to the corduroy trousers, a pair of extra thick drawers.

"You're lucky, Donald," Rob told the other, "for these corduroys would serve as a mighty good buffer; and, besides, you've had a pad in the other garment. Bad as your leg may be bruised, it would have been a whole lot worse only for these shields."

By this time he had bared the lower part of Donald's limb. The boy had his teeth clenched tightly together, as though necessarily there was more or less acute pain connected with this business; but it could not make him even wince, such was his astonishing grit. Andy surveyed him with renewed admiration, for if there was one thing that he liked to see it was this quality in a fellow. Andy himself was in the habit of also setting his teeth grimly when in pain and suppressing all groans.

As for Tubby, he stared as though he half believed he might be asleep and dreaming all this. He saw a dark black-and-blue bruise on the white skin of the boy's leg, halfway up to the knee. Doubtless there was another just like it on the opposite side. Tubby knew it must hurt like anything. He also wondered greatly what could have given such strange bruises. Then Rob, speaking, excited his curiosity still further.

"You see," said the scout master, as he started to gently rub some of the soothing salve on the leg of the Canadian boy, "if the springs of that trap had been new and vigorous instead of rusted out and weak, they might have broken the bone here. As it was, they just gripped you and held tight enough to keep you from breaking away, seeing that you couldn't possibly manage to get around so as to press down one of the springs."

"Trap!" ejaculated Tubby. "Oh, why don't you hurry up and explain it all to me, Andy Bowles? Rob, you tell me, won't you? What sort of a trap was this poor fellow caught in?"

"It was an old bear trap, you see, that his own cousin had set a while ago, thinking to make use of it, as he had seen the tracks of a big black bear over this way," Andy hastened to say. "Donald was hurrying along through the woods, never thinking about anything of this kind, when all at once he found himself caught. He's been held fast there for more than an hour, calling out for help as loudly as he could. He was in a desperate hurry to get across the line, because by accident he overheard some rascals scheming to blow up the railway bridge this very night."

"Great thunder!" was all Tubby could gasp, but the look on his face spoke volumes.

"That's pretty lively stuff, of course, Tubby," continued Andy, with the skill of a diplomat, "but the worst is yet to come; for, do you know, Donald's father is an engineer in the employ of the Canadian railway, and it happens that he pulls the munition train this very night, that these fiends are planning to destroy along with the bridge!"

Tubby was fairly holding his breath as he drank in all these amazing details. His round face began to grow furiously red with a riot of emotions that made his heart beat twice as fast as was its wont. Then, as if he dimly suspected that Andy, given to practical jokes, might be taking advantage of his confiding nature, Tubby turned toward the scout master and implored him to corroborate the story.

"Oh, *is* it all true, Rob?" he asked tremulously. "Would Andy be so mean as to deceive a trusting comrade in khaki? Please tell me, Rob!"

"Every word is just as he tells you, Tubby," said the other, still engaged in gently, but more vigorously than before, rubbing the discolored leg of the boy; and, singularly enough, it did not seem to hurt quite as much as at first, from which Donald must be inclined to believe there was considerable virtue in that "magical compound" as a pain remover and a balm in time of trouble.

"And are we going to stand by him, Rob, and try to break up the dastardly game of those criminal plotters?" continued Tubby.

"You give them a pretty hard name," laughed Rob. "I reckon they'd deny anything of that sort indignantly, saying anything is fair in war time. All the same, *we* believe they deserve to be called scoundrels. Yes, we mean to stand back of Donald, if that's what you mean, Tubby. We settled all that on the way here."

"Going over into Canada, and warn the bridge guards, you mean, Rob?"

"Nothing more or less," he was informed steadily. "Our only fear is that we may not get there in time to save the bridge."

"'Course we're all in this, Rob?" asked Tubby. "You wouldn't dream of asking *me* to stay behind, when anything of this sort was being pulled off? I've never balked when ordered to obey by a superior officer, but in such a case as this—well, you wouldn't treat me so mean as that, I just know it, Rob."

"Make yourself easy on that score," said Rob, wishing to relieve the strain of suspense under which he knew only too well Tubby was laboring. "We're all going, all but Wolf here, and we'll leave him behind to guard the cabin, with plenty of grub to keep him alive for a week. I hope that satisfies you, Tubby."

"Thank you, Rob; I'm more than glad to hear you say that. I never would have gotten over it if I'd been left in the lurch when this glorious stunt was being pulled off. I promise you that I'll keep up with the procession. Surely I can walk as fast as poor injured Donald here, who has such a game leg. Yes, I'm satisfied."

CHAPTER XV
ON DUTY BENT

About this time Rob ceased rubbing in the salve.

"There," he told Donald, as he helped the other draw down his trouser leg once more, "I've done all I can for the present. I'll take the salve along, and let you have another application later on, if you want me to; or it may be your good mother at home will have something just as fine."

Tubby had been impressed with the grit of the boy who had shown such a commendable spirit. He understood what Donald meant when he said he was bound to go along, no matter if he had to hobble, or even crawl a part of the way. Tubby thought that if this was a fair sample of the valiant fellows whom "Our Lady of the Snows," as Canada is often called, had sent across the sea, they would surely "do their bit" for the cause they believed was just.

"Oh, Rob, we forgot one thing!" suddenly exclaimed Tubby.

"What's that?" demanded Andy.

"Why, my uncle, you know, boys, will be coming back, perhaps before we return, and he won't know what to make of seeing our things here without a word of explanation."

"I've thought of that," said the scout leader promptly, nor was Tubby much surprised; it seemed as though Rob never forgot anything. "Sit down and write a few lines in a hurry, Tubby, while the rest of us finish what few preparations are still necessary. For one thing, I'm going to fill the lantern again, because the tank is pretty low and I've found a gallon of oil handy."

"But what shall I tell him?" asked the other, as he dropped upon a seat near the rude table on which were paper and pencil.

"Just say what's fetched us up here, and that you're going to leave the paper he's to sign. Then he can see that it gets back safe, in case anything should happen to keep us from returning here."

Tubby winced when he heard those words, they seemed so suggestive of some unknown peril threatening them. He kept on asking questions.

"I'd better say something about where we've gone, and why, hadn't I, Rob?"

"Yes, just as little as you can; and now get busy. We'll be ready to leave here in less than thirty shakes of a lamb's tail."

So Tubby started in. He may never have taken the prize for rapidity in penmanship and composition at school, for he was slow in everything he undertook, save eating. Spurred on by necessity which knows no law, he wrote hurriedly, telling in as few words as he could the "gist" of what was required. If any of the teachers in Hampton High could have watched Tubby as he sat there, with his tongue-tip between his teeth and a look of grim determination on his ruddy countenance, and witnessed how his pencil glided rapidly across the paper, they would have certainly believed the world was coming to an end, or at least that wonders never ceased, for Tubby could no longer be called "as slow as molasses in winter" or possessed of the characteristics of the creeping snail.

"There, that's done!" said the writer finally, with a sigh of relief. "I've made a bully good job of it, too, Rob—saying just enough without any superfluous language. I hope Uncle George doesn't destroy this message. I think it's a real gem, and as good as anything I ever did. I'd like to preserve it."

"Well, we're about ready," said Rob quickly. "Andy's got a snack of food to take along, so we may be prepared for emergencies."

"Oh, I hope now you don't dream that we'll get lost and wander all around in a dense Canadian bush for days!" exclaimed the alarmed Tubby.

"Not at all, with two such clever guides along," Rob told him. "You know preparedness is one of the cardinal virtues of every true scout. I never knew the time when some fellows would refuse to take a bite, especially after some hours of rough tramping."

They also saw to it that plenty of food was placed where the dog could secure it, for it was utterly out of the question for them to think of letting the animal accompany them. He might, by some inadvertent act, betray them at a time when it would mean unnecessary risk and trouble.

Tubby had placed the valuable paper and his explanatory missive on the table, so arranging them that they would catch the eye of his uncle as soon as the sportsman entered the bunk-house. Wolf had been fastened with a piece of rope, for it was not necessary that he should have the freedom of the place. Tubby was too tender-hearted to neglect a single thing in connection with the dog's comfort while they were absent. Accordingly, he had placed a bucket full of water within easy reach of the dog.

"Good-bye, old chap!" he told Wolf, and received a friendly bark in return. "We'll see you later, perhaps in the morning. Make yourself at home, and, above all things, be sure not to gorge too much. It's a bad thing to make a pig of yourself about eating, Wolf. I've known a human to come back for a fourth helping, when he could hardly breathe, and he was thin in the bargain, like you. So farewell, old Wolf, and take things easy while we're gone."

At another time Andy might have flared up because of this direct allusion to his particular failing, and declared that he "was not the only pebble on the beach" when it came to "stuffing," but there was so much of a more thrilling nature to occupy his mind that he let it go by, just as water might run off a duck's back.

They passed outside, and the door was fastened with the bar. Wolf barked several times, and there was a note of wonder in his dog language, as though he could not at all understand what it meant. Then Tubby heard plain sounds from within that told him his warning had fallen on deaf ears, for Wolf was already starting in to have a glorious feast, after which he would probably lie down contentedly and indulge in a sound sleep; nor would he mind being left alone as long as the food supply held out—he was only a dog, you see, with a dog's nature.

"Good-bye, old shack!" said Tubby, who seemed to have a streak of sentiment in his make-up, considerably more so than either of his mates. "We've certainly enjoyed you as long as we were here, and hope to see you again soon. Ta-ta!"

"Oh, let up on all that talk, Tubby!" complained Andy. "I really believe you love to hear yourself speak. If there's anything worth while to say, it isn't so bad. Better save your wind, because you'll need it unless all the signs fail."

Tubby, knowing that these were really words of wisdom, managed to "bottle up" as he was directed. Indeed, once they had commenced to thread the mazes of the forest he found that he had all he could do to follow the lead of the lame boy who served as guide to the expedition. All sorts of obstacles lay in the way, and it seemed as though most of these took especial delight in getting under Tubby's feet. He had to dodge snags, climb over logs, brush through bushes that plucked his campaign hat from his head and scratched his face, slide down into miniature gullies, and then painfully climb up the opposite side; and all these various "ups and downs" kept repeating themselves over and over again.

But Tubby was "dead game." He had entreated to be allowed to accompany this expedition across the line, and no matter what happened, his chums would never hear a complaint from his lips, not if he died in the endeavor to "keep up with the procession."

Shame alone would have kept Tubby from showing any sign of weakness. He knew Donald must be suffering agonies from that sorely injured leg of his, for Tubby watched him limp at times when he forgot himself and half drag that limb after him. Well, it would be disgusting, according to Tubby's notion, for a well and hearty fellow of his build to let a game little Canadian chap, with a bruised leg in the bargain, leave him in the lurch.

So they moved on, Rob had lighted the refilled lantern, believing that while there was no danger of their being discovered it was wise to have it burning, for the illumination, while scant in its way, might prove a time-saver. This allowed them to see what obstacles lay in their path, for which Tubby was very thankful; it undoubtedly saved him many a stumble, and possibly not a few bruises.

Big Zeb followed behind Rob, who was second, and Andy came between the woods guide and Tubby. In this order they were strung out along the zigzag path which, thin as it was through less frequent use in these days since the loggers had gone, could evidently be easily discovered by the sharp vision of the young Canadian scout.

This grouping also allowed Rob to hold occasional communication with Donald or Zeb, as the inclination or the necessity arose. After they had been going for some time Rob thought it well to find out whether Zeb agreed with the course along which the engineer's son was leading them.

"I don't suppose, Zeb," he said softly, "that you chance to know of any shorter way for crossing the International Boundary?"

"No, I don't know," admitted the big guide. "He's goin' as straight as the flight o' an arrow for the line. I knows this here path. Many a time have I gone along it, with Mr. Hopkins, who wasn't mindin' much which side o' the line he got his moose on, so long as nobody bothered him. An' some o' the border patrols could be fixed to wink at that sort o' thing; because the moose, ye see, passed from one side to the other right along. Yes, we're gettin' tha, younker, as neat as ye please. Donald sure knows what he's adoin'."

This was comforting news for Rob. It also pleased the others. When there is much need for accuracy two heads are often better than one, especially when in full accord.

Tubby figuratively "shook hands with himself" when he heard this, for it served to allay his last lingering suspicion that Rob feared they might get lost in the wilderness.

Although the fact has not been thus far mentioned, it can be taken for granted that the party left none of their firearms behind them at the logging camp when they started forth upon this dangerous mission. They did not know positively that any occasion would arise when the possession of these weapons would save them a world of trouble. Since they were about to compete with desperate plotters, who would naturally be armed, every one believed it was good policy to be ready to defend themselves in an emergency. As Rob said, "when you're in Rome you've got to do as the Romans do."

"How far from the logging camp would you say the border lies, Donald?" asked Rob, after more time had passed.

"Not more than two full miles alang this path," came the answer.

"Right, to the dot!" commented Zeb.

"But surely we've come nearly that far by now," Tubby up and said from the rear, as he ducked under some bushes that developed a fondness for scratching his face.

"We are nearly there," asserted the guide, and then Andy hastily exclaimed:

"Listen, boys! that sounds like the rumble of a train right now in the near distance!"

"Oh! horrors!" gasped Tubby. "Can it be that we're too late, after all?"

CHAPTER XVI
THE STONE CAIRN ON THE BORDER

"Naw, naw, ye're baith wrang!" hastily exclaimed Donald, as soon as he could "get a word in edgewise."

"But that certainly was a train we heard," affirmed Andy stoutly, adding: "There goes a whistle! Don't you hear it, Donald?"

"Oh, ay, but ye ken it was not my fayther's hand at the throttle of the engine. That train is the regular passenger goin' west. It is much too airly for the freight carrying munitions and stores, and bound east."

"Well, I'm glad to hear you say so," Andy was quick to admit.

"I can breathe easy again," muttered Tubby, who had received quite a severe shock.

The sound of the train grew louder. They could even tell when it struck out on the trestle that served as an approach for the long and costly bridge. Naturally it thrilled them to remember that the unworthy plot of those who would strike a cowardly blow at the enemy of their native country by abusing the neutrality of the land that gave them friendly shelter—and protected them in the bargain—that this plan was laid to destroy that splendid piece of mechanical engineering, and, perhaps, engulf many human beings in the wreckage.

"Everything seems to be right—so far," observed Andy, as they once again started to hurry along the dimly seen trail.

"We ought to be in time," Donald told them over his shoulder, "accordin' to what I heard them say. It's hopin' and prayin' I am that I can hold out to the end. If the worst does come, why here's a braw chap who could tak ye to the bridge. A' ye hae to do is to tell them that Donald, the engineer's lad, sent ye with the warnin'. They'll know what to do the nicht. But I'll manage somehow to get there, by hook or by crook."

"You certainly will, if being game counts for anything, Donald, old fellow," Andy assured him. "I never ran across a scout with more grit than you're showing right now. Why, nearly any boy, with such a badly bruised leg, would be glad to let some one else do the running for him, satisfied to get the glory himself."

"But do ye not understand, I could nae do anything less, because it is my ain fayther whose life is in danger?" the other said, apparently thinking that he was doing nothing so very wonderful—nothing more than any boy ought to do for the parent he loved.

The train was going away from them now, and by degrees they heard the sound of its passage less distinctly, until presently the rumble became very faint indeed, and then died away completely, though the falling of the night wind may have had considerable to do with this.

Rob, being a scout who always paid attention to even the smallest details, when on duty or off, for it had become second-nature with him, noticed that they were just about exactly opposite the place where, from the deep rumble, it seemed the western trestle and approach must lie. This he also knew was the end of the bridge they were heading for, since to reach the other terminus it would first of all be necessary to cross the river, which they were not prepared to do.

Besides, it was absolutely certain that the conspirators would also approach the object they planned to destroy from this side; and consequently Rob meant to extinguish the lantern, once he learned they were across the line.

"I can see something queer, like a pile of stones, ahead there," announced Andy, who had particularly keen eyesight, and chanced to be looking forward at the time, instead of minding his steps.

"It is the cairn that marks the boundary," said the Canadian boy simply.

A minute later and they had approached so close that all of them could easily see the object, which turned out to be a heaped-up pile of rocks, and on top was a broad stone slab, with some markings on it. Looking closer at the "monument" the boys read the words: "Boundary Line," and underneath this "United States." On the other side they discovered the word "Canada" below the same descriptive text.

"Well," said Tubby, as they paused for a minute before crossing over, "just to think that I can sit here on this rock-pile, with one foot over in a foreign country and the other in our own home land. It seems queer!"

"Huh!" grunted Andy, always ready for a sly fling at good-natured Tubby, "take care then that you don't have to sit on a stone-pile day after day, and wearing a striped suit. Please don't get the habit, Tubby."

"I won't, I promise you," retorted the other, "for it might be catching, like the measles, and you'd be a fit subject for contagion, Andy."

"Start on, Donald," said Rob, as he deliberately blew out the lantern, which he proceeded to carefully deposit at the base of the little pyramid of rocks, where they could get it again when on their way back to camp.

Evidently Rob did not believe there would be any further necessity for carrying a lantern. Besides, it was more or less of an encumbrance, since he had his rifle to handle in the bargain.

Tubby did not wholly like this. It would probably mean more frequent stumbles for him, and also knocks and scratches; but he did not remonstrate, knowing well that Rob was the best judge of what was right and proper.

So they all crossed the border, and found themselves treading the soil of Canada, for the first time in the lives of the three Boy Scouts of Hampton Troop.

"Why, it doesn't seem one whit different," said Tubby, in evident surprise, "and only for that sign on the slab of rock I'd never dream that I'd stepped over from Uncle Sam's world, and was treading foreign soil."

Andy was heard to snort as though highly amused, but he resisted the temptation to take a fling at the "unsophisticated farmer," as he sometimes called simple-minded Tubby. As though there would be any perceptible difference in the soil and trees and rocks, because an imaginary line divided the continent between two entirely different nations!

Tubby sometimes knew better than he made out, and perhaps Andy was wise not to pursue the subject any further; he had been "stung" before, when attempting to take advantage of a "break" on the part of amiable Tubby.

"After this," Rob was telling them, "be careful not to talk so loud. We don't know which trail those men may take in passing across the border; but if they heard us speaking they would become suspicious at once. You must know that the very desperate character of their work would make them think everybody's hand was raised against them; and the chances are they'd feel inclined to pounce on us, and at least make us prisoners."

"Oh, that must never be!" said Donald, with deep feeling. "If they kept us fra warnin' the bridge guards, ye ken, the whole thing wud be in the soup."

After that they all fell silent, and the forward progress was carried out as so many ghostly specters in a country churchyard might stalk about at the hour of twelve, if, indeed, such visitors from the other world ever do visit this one.

For one thing the path actually seemed to be growing easier now, Tubby thought. At least he did not meet with so many obstacles to his progress, and could thank his lucky stars on this account. He really believed every square inch of his stout limbs below his knees must by now show signs of having come in rough contact with stumps, logs, rocks and all other manner of things. Indeed, Tubby had already made up his mind to apply in person to Rob for a portion of that healing salve, when a fitting opportunity arrived and their mission had been carried through successfully.

All of them listened anxiously as they went along. If a bird or a squirrel moved amidst the pine needles or the branches of a neighboring tree the sound, faint though it might be, gave them a corresponding thrill, because their nerves were all on edge, so to speak. Had a deer, lying in a thicket, suddenly bounded away with a crash of the undergrowth, Tubby feared he would faint, it was apt to give him such a terrible shock.

But there was no such alarm, and they were making steady progress all the while. Rob, as a rule, mapped out his plan of campaign beforehand, and he would have done so in this particular case also, only he considered that the honor of giving the warning should belong to Donald. The devoted

Canadian boy had made a gallant attempt to carry the news of his terrible discovery to those in charge of the bridge's safety; he had suffered all manner of pain and hardship in the effort, and it seemed only fair that he should reap most of the reward.

Besides, Donald knew the lay of the land in the vicinity of the bridge. Without his assistance as pilot to the expedition they might have strayed from the path and lost so much valuable time that even though they eventually arrived it would be only in time to hear the stunning report that would tell them the bridge was destroyed, and that the trainload of munitions had gone down into the gulf, a twisted mass of wreckage.

Tubby had conceived a new and somewhat alarming thought, and he wished that Rob had not placed that embargo on speech, for he wanted to ask a question very much. As it was, he had to take it out in looking anxiously upward every time they happened to be in an open bit of ground, where one could glimpse the clear heavens overhead, by straining the muscles of his neck terribly.

The fact of the matter was, Tubby had remembered about the aeroplane which all of them had so earnestly watched on that other day, when it sped across the line, descending low enough for the pilot to snap off a series of pictures of the ground below, together with the long railway bridge, and then once more scuttled away, heading for the American side of the border. He wondered whether those who meant to undertake the destruction of the bridge would come again in an aerial craft, and try to drop bombs upon the bridge at the moment the freight from the west was approaching the trestle.

Now, this was not so ridiculous as it might appear to some readers who may not know that Tubby, together with Rob and Merritt Crawford, had been abroad on the battlefields of Belgium and Northern France, where it was even then, in the early stages of the war, a common occurrence for aviators to soar over supply depots, railway stations, and various other central points, to try and blow them up by bombs they let fall from a great height. Why, Tubby could remember having looked upon a church used as an observation tower that had been successfully bombed in that way by a daring Teuton aviator.

He took a little more comfort, however, when presently he remembered that Donald had heard the plotters going over the details of their plans, and that according to all that was then said, they very evidently meant to use dynamite, planted under the trestle, and fired by means of a long copper insulated wire and a battery.

Plodding on, the little party began to ascend what seemed to be a gradual rise of ground. This would indicate that they were drawing near the railway line, for it was on a high bank at this place, a necessity caused by the fact of having to cross the river close by.

Tubby wondered what the next half-hour was fated to bring forth. He hoped they were going to meet with the success their efforts deserved, and that the miserable scheme might be nipped in the bud. Tired as the stout youth certainly must be, he was yet buoyed up by the excitement that had him in its clutches; and though the threatened bridge had been twice as far distant Tubby stood ready to keep going until he dropped from sheer exhaustion.

But the time was coming when the dull monotony of that advance was fated to be abruptly broken, and in a way calculated to give them a fresh thrill.

CHAPTER XVII
LYNX LAW

Donald had asked anxiously several times how the night was going. As a scout he might possibly have been able to tell this fairly well by the position of the heavenly bodies, particularly the planets; for every scout is supposed to include this woodsman's trick in his education before he can call himself fit to wander at will in an unknown wilderness. But then Donald was hardly in a condition to depend on himself, and so he several times whispered to Rob:

"Is it gitting alang toward eleven, wud ye mind tellin' me?"

It was still far from that, but evidently the particular hour Donald mentioned was wearing upon his mind, and he took counsel from his fears. Rob concluded that the long and heavily-laden munition freight was due at the bridge about eleven. And at the steady progress they were making he felt pretty certain they would be in ample time to give warning, unless something cropped up to detain them, which Rob fervently hoped would not be the case.

Tubby was still clinging to the rear, but doing nobly—for him. Even Andy felt a tinge of justifiable pride in the work of the stout chum, because he knew what a handicap Tubby always labored under when energy and sustained effort had to be looked to in order to pull one through. It meant a whole lot more for Tubby to accomplish this swift tramp than to any one of the other fellows, injured Donald alone excepted.

If he puffed and wheezed occasionally that was no more than might be expected. Every time Andy glanced over his shoulder on missing these familiar sounds, a faint fear oppressing him that the other had fallen out of line, he discovered the stout chum in motion not far back of his heels.

"Bully for Tubby; he's all right!" Andy was saying to himself, for really he had a deep and abiding affection for the good-natured one, even though addicted to "rubbing it in" occasionally, when an evil spirit moved him to play practical jokes.

Then it happened!

Donald came to a sudden halt, and uttered a low but disgusted grunt.

"What's the matter; lost the trail?" whispered Rob, for that was the first and most natural explanation that appealed to him.

"We're in hard luck, I ken!" muttered the pilot of the expedition.

"In what way?" demanded Rob.

"It's a muckle sair job, wi' that awfu' creature barrin' the way. If ye look, Rab, ye can see his yellow eyes gleamin' up yonder in the tree. The beastie is crouchin' on a lower limb, and right o'er the trail. He will nae let us pass by, I fear me."

All of them heard what Donald said, and every pair of eyes was immediately turned toward the place just ahead that he indicated. Sure enough something glowed in the semi-darkness, something that seemed like twin spots of phosphorus, about eight feet or so from the ground, and in conjunction with the lower limb of the big, bushy hemlock.

Even Tubby knew that only the orbs of the feline or cat species could display such glaring eyes in the night-time.

"Wow! a bobcat!" exclaimed Andy, fussing with his gun, though Rob instantly laid a detaining hand on his arm and hastily remarked:

"None of that sort of work, Andy, on your life, remember! It would ruin the whole business with us! It's a dangerous job to try to shoot a cat when you can only see the glare of its eyes. Donald, what do you say?"

"First then, it is no common cat, but a big lynx, a fearsome creature for any man to tackle," returned the young Canadian with complete assurance that told he knew what he was speaking about.

"Worse and worse!" grunted Andy, feeling a trifle disappointed because Rob had laid down the law, for he aspired to some day kill such a fighting monster as a full-grown Canada lynx, and it was too bad that circumstances over which he had no control were now fated to keep him from carrying out that somewhat ambitious desire.

Rob had been fumbling about his person, and suddenly there shot out a small but intense ray of light. The scout master had thought to fetch along with him that exceedingly useful little hand electric torch, and was now putting the same to good service.

Tubby stood on his tiptoes in order to see better, for he chanced to be just behind Andy, who somehow did not think to step aside. What he beheld gave him a further quiver along the region of his spine, as Tubby afterward admitted "just as if some malicious joker had suddenly emptied a bucketful of icy water down his back."

There was no mistake about it. Crouching upon the limb of the hemlock they could see the beast, much larger than any wildcat they had ever met in all their travels, and plainly marked with odd-looking tasselated ears, and the hairy growth so like whiskers, that distinguish the true Canadian lynx.

The cat did not like that piercing glow from Rob's dazzling light as was evidenced by a low fierce growling sound. Tubby had often heard the pet tomcat at home make that same noise when holding a captured sparrow between his teeth, and threatened by a rival and envious feline desirous of taking the prize away from the possessor.

At the same time the lynx showed no disposition to retreat, while they would not dare venture along the trail, because in so doing they must pass directly under its "roost," as Andy called it.

Besides, Rob was not without caution, though on occasion he could be just as dashing as the next one. There was always a time when discretion might be deemed the better part of valor; and such an occasion now confronted them, Rob thought.

Donald, poor fellow, was figuratively speaking on "needles and pins," what with his impatience to get on, and his knowledge of the dauntless habits of the animal that now disputed their right to that trail.

"There's only one thing we can do," said Rob decisively, for he was a great believer in "taking the bull by the horns," or cutting the Gordian knot when it could not be untied, just as Alexander the Great is said to have done on occasion. "We must turn aside, and go around the brute. Let him stay in the tree where he is, if that's his game. All we want is to get along, and lose no more time than is necessary."

Andy was heard to give a sigh. How he did hate to "knuckle down" to a miserable old lynx that considered them trespassers on his domain, and perhaps knew they were just invading Yankee boys who had crossed the line despite the law that forbade trespass on the part of foreigners.

"A gude idea, Rab!" exclaimed Donald, overjoyed. "Mair strength to yer elbow, man. And let us gang awa' without anny more bother."

"Oh, well, all right," grumbled Andy, in a disgusted tone. "It's hard lines, let me tell you."

Tubby was not saying anything, but he did a heap of staring. He noticed that as they left the trail and began to make a half circle so as to pass around the big hemlock containing that audacious lynx, Rob continued to play his electric torch so that its glow fell upon the crouching beast. There was a double object in this, for not only could they keep watch over the animal, and feel assured it had not left that limb to follow them; but at the same time the lynx would have to remain under the mystic spell of the glowing orb that dazzled it.

Andy kept his gun in readiness, for he was determined that should the beast make any attempt at attacking them he could not be bound by any order which would prevent him from shooting. But there was no occasion for violence. The lynx twisted its head around so as to follow their passage, but when last seen it had not even changed its position on the limb. As Tubby told himself half humorously it "just seemed bent on seeing a disreputable rabble well off the premises," when it could once more take up the necessary duty of securing a dinner.

Tubby was also concerned in casting his eyes about him in momentary expectation of discovering another pair of glowing eyes amidst the tangle of branches above; for he remembered that most cats hunt in couples, often surrounding their game. He was looking for the mate of the lynx in the hemlock, looking, but at the same time fervently praying that it would only be conspicuous by reason of its absence, for Tubby was not at all fond of any sort of cats, domestic or wild.

All of them breathed sighs of satisfaction when they could no longer see any sign of the ferocious four-footed hunter of the trail. Rob had now extinguished his light, for he did not wish to needlessly exhaust the little battery; it had already proven worth its price, and was likely to come in handy on still further occasions in the near future.

"Not much danger of his following after us, I suppose, Donald?" Rob asked softly. He felt that the Canadian boy must be much better acquainted with the characteristics of such a native animal than he could boast of being.

"Na, I dinna think so. The beastie is satisfied to see us go around and leave him in possession. He is nae lookin' after the likes o' us just noo. But I hae another trouble facin' me."

"You mean finding the trail again, don't you, Donald?" asked Rob.

"Just so," came the reply. "I know the general direction we must be goin' till we reach the railway, but it wud be so much better if we were able to continue alang the path."

"We turned off to the right," said the observing scout master, "and so it is bound to lie over on our left. You could tell when you struck it, I suppose, Donald?"

"Oh! ay, if on'y I could *see*," the pilot assured him.

"Well, we'll soon fix that part of it easy enough," remarked Rob, and once more he had recourse to his invaluable vest pocket edition of a hand torch.

He and Donald walked side by side, using their eyes to the best advantage as they slowly advanced. Rob, being a clever woodsman, could pick out a trail that had been frequently used by passing human beings and animals, even though he may never have previously set eyes on the spot himself. As for Donald, surely he ought to be able to equal the cousin scout from over the border, for he was quite at home in these Canadian woods.

Andy, not being able to assist, was well contented to follow after those in the lead, and let them shoulder all the responsibility. Andy had a little weakness in this direction, which sometimes cropped up; and many boys are apt to think it a good thing when they can get some one else to assume all the care, while on their part they go "scot free."

Tubby was beginning to worry. He fancied they might have "rough sledding" ahead of them. Why, this even began to look a little as though they were getting lost; at any rate, the *trail* was lost, which amounted to nearly the same thing. So Tubby was feeling that queer sensation again in the region of his heart, which had begun to pump doubly fast. Tubby's naturally timorous nature had never been fully conquered, and there were plenty of occasions when it gave him much trouble. He feared lest he might be disgraced in the eyes of his chums by appearing a coward, something he sincerely detested.

Several precious minutes passed. In vain did Tubby listen to hear either of the trail hunters declare that their efforts had met with success.

"Yes, I guess after all we must be lost!" the stout scout began to admit to himself forlornly; and, indeed, it looked rather serious.

CHAPTER XVIII
THE TRAIL TO THE TRESTLE

"It's certainly queer where that trail can be," Rob himself was saying. On hearing this Tubby's heart took on an additional flutter, for he seemed to think things must be pretty serious when experienced Rob, who seldom allowed himself to show the least sign of discouragement, should speak in this strain.

"We hae already come twicet as far as I thought wud be necessary," admitted Donald, "and naething yet o' the pesky thing."

"I'm dead sure we haven't passed over it," added the scout master. "While one pair of eyes might have failed two could hardly have been deceived. There's only one explanation that I can think of."

"Oh! what's that, Rob?" hastily asked Tubby, making a great effort to keep that miserable tremor from affecting his voice, though he felt that he just *had* to say something.

"The trail must have taken a sudden bend just about that big hemlock," Rob explained. "You've been over it so many times, Donald, I should think you might remember whether it does."

"It's verra curious," spoke up Donald reflectively, "but I gie ye my word I was thinkin' the same thing this minute. I am beginning to believe that it does the thing, ye ken. If that be so, then a' we hae to do is to keep on goin' till we fetch up once mair on the trail."

"Well, let's make an agreement," said Rob. "We'll keep along for five minutes, and if nothing shows up it would be better for us to abandon all hope of running across the path. Then we will have to shape our course as best we may, with both you and Zeb here to figure things out. There's no doubt about our hitting the railway embankment somehow."

"It is unco' kind o' ye to say that, Rab!" declared the Canadian lad, who blessed the lucky chance that had raised up such devoted and loyal friends as these cousins from over the border, when he was more in need of help than ever before in all his young life.

"Why not call on Zeb here to give his opinion, Rob?" mentioned Andy, having a sudden bright thought. It occurred to him that a veteran woodsman's advice ought to be particularly valuable under such conditions as now confronted them.

"How foolish o' us not to hae thought o' that before," said Donald contritely.

"Better late than never," muttered Andy.

Rob, turning upon the big guide, hastened to say: "Zeb, you understand how it is, and why we haven't bothered mentioning this before. Donald was supposed to know more about this region than any one else; but now he is up a stump, and perhaps you could help us out. So please tell us, if you know about this part of the country, and particularly this trail we've been following."

"Wall, I sartin do have reason for rememberin' that same big hemlock the cat was squattin' in," he said. Apparently the rough Maine woods guide was not cherishing any resentment because he had not been considered in the matter.

"It was under that tree Mr. Hopkins he shot the best moose bull he ever got. That was three winters ago. We was follerin' this path, when he broke cover and went down all in a heap at the fust shot. Say, but Mr. Hopkins he was some proud o' that shot, fur it took right behind the shoulder, and tumbled the big bull over inside o' twenty yards."

"Try and remember, Zeb, about the trail; forget all those other things. Did it make a twist and a turn somewhere about that hemlock?" asked Rob.

"It sartinly did, sir," the guide assured him. "I remember it because we had occasion to look fur water, an' hearin' a stream nigh by I went on to scout for it. Yes, the path made a quick bend at the hemlock. It took up the old direction arter a bit."

"That settles it," remarked Rob, fully satisfied. "We go on further, and I expect we'll soon run across our trail."

"Good enough," grunted Andy. "Nothing like corroborative evidence. Donald *thought* he was right, and now we *know* he was, as sure as shooting."

"That'll do, Andy," cautioned Rob, who feared they were all doing more talking than discretion allowed. Who could say what hostile ears might not be within hearing distance, hidden by that semi-darkness surrounding them on every side?

They started on. Hardly had two minutes passed, fraught with untold anxiety to at least one of the party, Tubby, when Donald was heard to give a low exclamation. This time there was a note of joy and not dismay permeating the cry.

"Have you struck it, Donald?" whispered Andy, close behind the others.

"Faith, an' I hae done that, laddie," bubbled the Scotch-Canadian boy, so filled with delight that he could hardly refrain from shaking hands with each of his companions.

Rob saw that it was even so, for his quick and practiced eye told him the trail lay before them, as seen in the glow of the hand torch.

"We'll have to douse the glim from now on," he announced. "Much as I'd prefer to keep up its use, for we could go faster, it might be seen by someone, and bring us more trouble than we'd care to face."

He shut off the light. It looked doubly gloomy to Tubby, once they had to depend wholly on the dim glow of the stars above, for bright as these heavenly bodies may appear, they afford but a poor substitute for a torch, backed by a little electric battery with its illumination focussed at one point.

"I hope we don't lose it again," ventured Tubby, who had sighed with relief at the luck that came their way. He had come very near saying, "I hope we don't get lost again," but caught himself in the nick of time.

"There is verra little danger o' that, I assure ye," Donald told him, as once more he started bravely forth.

Thus far Donald had managed to keep going, though Rob could not help noticing that the effort was beginning to tell upon him seriously. That limp of his cropped up more frequently than at first; indeed, if the boy took his mind off the subject for a brief space of time he was sure to fall into stumbling along. Rob hoped he would be able to hold out to the end. At the same time he had made up his mind he and Andy, and Zeb, perhaps, would finish the mission of warning the guards, even though it became necessary to leave Donald behind, with Tubby to keep him company. He had never undertaken a task that appealed more to him than this stand for neutrality. There was something strangely fascinating about it, something uplifting, that appealed to Rob strongly. He felt that he was doing his full duty as a patriotic citizen of the great United States, in thus attempting to foil the miserable and pernicious schemes of those plotters who, if only they could accomplish their plan for injuring the Allies, did not care how much they embroiled Uncle Sam with his northern neighbor and the world at war.

"I saw something then that looked a whole lot like the flash of a match," suddenly muttered the quick-seeing Andy.

"It was a match," admitted Rob. "I saw it, too. From the fact that it seemed to be higher up than we are I take it the man who struck it must have been a guard on the railway embankment, in which case it is only a short distance from us now."

"But why would he want to strike a match, please?" asked Tubby, pushing his head close up to the others in his burning desire to learn facts and theories.

"Oh, perhaps just to light his pipe," returned Rob, whispering, of course. "Fact is that must have been just what he was doing. I saw the light flare up several times, and that would mean so many puffs. These Canadians, like the British, are great hands for a pipe, you know."

"Let us be awa' then," urged Donald feverishly. "Tell me, please, Rab, is it yet near the hour o' eleven?"

He could hardly have exhibited more eagerness had he heard the far distant rumble that would announce the coming of his father's train. Ere this the poor boy was in a real fever, brought on by his emotions, as well as the nature of his recent severe exposure and physical suffering.

Rob understood all this and could sympathize with Donald. At the same time he also knew they were now about to approach the real danger that overhung the adventure. Undoubtedly those desperate men must be near by at work, intent on carrying out their monstrous scheme that would entail so much loss of property and life. So, in trying to communicate with the guards of the trestle and the adjacent bridge, they would have to run the gantlet of discovery at the hands of the dynamiters.

"Plenty of time yet, Donald," Rob said in the ear of the eager one. "Many a fine plan has been spoiled by too great haste. We'll carry it through to a successful finish. This won't be the first time the scouts of the Eagle Patrol have been put on their mettle. Donald, they have always won out. Wait and see."

"Rob," ventured Andy, in his most muffled tones, "I just *know* you've got a bully good plan up your sleeve right now. Tell us what it is, won't you?"

"Get your heads close together, then," cautioned the scout master.

When they had done this he went on:

"Donald, you ought to know all about this trestle here, since you've been around it many a time. Am I right?"

"I thought I had tawld ye I did before, Rab."

"All right. Then try to decide, if you can, just where these men would be most apt to lay their mine. You can figure that out, can't you, Donald?"

The other stopped to think it over carefully, for he was beginning to grasp the tremendous idea that had taken hold upon the intrepid scout master.

"Ay, there is one place above a' ithers they wud select. I gie ye my word on it, Rab. The mair I think o' it the stronger that appeals to me. An' if the mine were exploded underneath the trestle it wud do jist as much damage as though the bridge itsel' were toppled down. An' the train,—my soul, what an awfu' fall there would be!"

Small wonder if the boy shivered as he said this. It must be remembered his one thought lay in the fact that the engineer whose hand would be on the throttle of that ill-fated locomotive was his own dearly beloved father.

"All right, then, Donald, we want you to lead us as straight to that particular spot as you can in this darkness. When we strike the trestle we will all start to getting down on our hands and knees, and feeling for something in the way of a trailing copper insulated wire."

Andy gave a little snort of delight as he grasped the idea.

"Fine, Rob!" he whispered. "You mean to cut the connections, don't you? When they press down the button of their old battery, expecting to fire the hidden mine, why, nothing will follow! It's a sure enough bully scheme."

Tubby felt like hugging himself, or Rob, or some one, he hardly cared who, for just as always happened, Rob was proving himself to be master of circumstances. Oh! he had seen Rob carry out so many schemes built on this order that Tubby knew success was bound to come to them again.

"Come awa' then," urged Donald, and Rob only added:

"No whispering after this, unless you put your lips directly up to my ear."

So they crept cautiously forward, and inside of three minutes Tubby began to see the trestle work looming up between himself and the sky. They had apparently reached the crisis in their fateful affair.

CHAPTER XIX
THE HUNT FOR THE WIRE

While it was thus possible to make out the faint tracery of the high trestle and its attendant bridge, objects were not so very plain after all; and even youthful eyes had to undergo considerable of a strain in order to succeed at all.

Remembering what Rob had said with regard to their object in searching for the wire that would in all likelihood run between the hidden mine and the lurking place of the plotters, every one was excessively vigilant. It might happen that with great luck they would be able to discover this connecting link in the start. Such a piece of good fortune would simplify matters wonderfully, for they understood just what the intentions of the scout master were.

In a nutshell, then, to make the facts plain to the reader in the start, they anticipated severing connections so that when the fatal moment arrived and the lawless breakers of neutrality sought to consummate their act, they would not meet with any sort of success, for with the conductor of the electric current broken the mine could not be exploded.

They had not gone very far, always approaching closer to the embankment near by the commencement of the trestle, when Rob stopped short. Every one had the customary thrill; indeed, that would hardly apply because one of these little spasms seemed to follow so close upon the heels of another that they were in an almost constant state of apprehension.

Rob must have made some sort of discovery or he would not have called a halt in this fashion. Donald was at his side now, and had also come to a pause, so the others brushed up against them, making a compact clump as they crouched there, and strained all their faculties.

Now, the three members of the old Eagle Patrol had been together so much, and passed through so many adventures in common, that long since they had agreed on a system of signals whereby they could communicate without any outsider being aware of what was going on. Thus a faint twitter, resembling a sleepy bird protesting at being pushed on its perch, would indicate that something had been seen that ought to be taken into consideration. A low grunt, after the manner of a hedgehog hunting for succulent roots, meant that retreat would be in order, though to be undertaken with the utmost circumspection.

There were a number of other ways in which the scouts could communicate without anyone being the wiser. Rob's warning indicated that he had made a discovery, which they, too, would be able to hit upon if they used their ears to the best advantage.

Ah! now it came stealing up to them. Even Tubby knew that it was not the grumble of a burrowing animal, but the low mutter of a hoarse, excited voice. It came but faintly at best, and certainly would never reach the hearing of any one located several times as far away as the crouching boys and Zeb were at the time.

Accustomed to practicing such things as the scouts were, they had no difficulty at all in picking out the exact spot from which this hoarse whisper came. Even Tubby could do that, for he was far from a tenderfoot, having been in harness quite as long as his two mates.

This tell-tale whisper informed them where the men whom they had set out to balk, were hiding. Yes, it was far enough away from the railway embankment to allow them to escape any possible evil results when the climax arrived and the mine was sprung, and yet sufficiently close to let them see the train as it swung down upon the high trestle, perhaps slowing up for the passage of the bridge.

Rob made a mental calculation as quick as a flash. He was thus enabled to get his bearings, and could figure out just about how that wire was likely to run. Thus it was possible, by making a little half-circuit, for them to cut across the line midway between the two ends, or perhaps still closer to the trestle. This would increase their own peril in case events moved more swiftly than they had been calculating.

Even more than at any previous time the utmost secrecy was necessary. Tubby felt that he was placed on his mettle. A stumble now would excite suspicion, and that, in turn, might influence the wary schemers, fearful of being caught. Rather than have their evil plans balked they would naturally prefer to explode the mine even before the train arrived.

Rob may have considered Tubby's customary clumsiness, and made provision to take as little chance as possible. That would be the natural conclusion to be drawn from the fact that he now sank still lower, until on his hands and knees, and in this ungainly but practical position they were all creeping along.

Tubby heard that low grumble of a fretful, impatient voice no longer. Perhaps the incautious member of the invading party had been suppressed by a fierce shove. Tubby wondered if their presence in the vicinity could have been discovered, or even suspected. He was preparing his nerves against a sudden terrific roar, as the valuable railway property came crashing down. He also fervently hoped that none of the heavy timbers would carry over to where they were creeping along.

Tubby was not feeling over-happy, but nothing would have induced the boy to forego the excitement. Perhaps, his nature being slow, Tubby might hold back longer than such impetuous fellows as Andy and some of the other Eagles. Once he enlisted in an undertaking he could not be easily "frozen out."

Rob had evidently gone as far in a line parallel with the trestle as he intended. He commenced to gradually swing around. He was bent on making that half-circuit, so as to cross the direct line of communication between the hiding place of the plotters and the railway.

They faced the west from this point on. That fact might seem of little moment, and yet it proved its value, for only because their faces were turned in that direction did they make a sudden discovery.

Something far distant was creeping up the heavens. It looked like a faint line of fire, and only for the fact that it mounted higher and higher instead of descending, Tubby would have believed it to be one of those erratic shooting stars or meteors, such as he had, like all boys, frequently watched darting athwart a summer sky at night-time.

But this was something quite different. Tubby guessed its nature even while the fiery finger still crept upward toward its zenith. It was a sky-rocket. Some patriotic Canadian was celebrating, for some cause or other, though Tubby did not happen to remember whether this was King George's birthday, or the anniversary of the late lamented Edward's natal day. Possibly good news had been received from across the sea. The stanch Canadian soldiers in the war trenches might have once more covered themselves with glory, and— then Tubby felt as though a frozen hand had come in contact with his heart, such was the mighty shiver that ran through his system. He had suddenly conceived another and more significant fact.

Why should that not be a signal rocket? He remembered that when abroad with his two chums, and visiting the French in the trenches, they had seen such fiery tracery against the night heavens, and understood that some commander was giving his orders; or else a spy far back of the enemy's lines was trying to communicate some important information he had picked up.

That altered the complexion of everything, Tubby thought. These desperate men must realize what a tremendous, as well as dangerous, job they had undertaken; and consequently they would try to cover every possibility, so there might be no fluke or miscarriage of their plans.

Yes, they undoubtedly had some trusty confederate waiting at a certain station on the railway, miles to the west, whose duty it was to signal them the fact that the million-dollar munition train had just left that point, and could be expected at the bridge within a certain time, which information would allow them to have everything prepared for the grand spectacular event.

They had neglected nothing, apparently, except taking into consideration the fact that a few members of the Eagle Patrol of Boy Scouts chanced to be up in that particular section of country at the time and, as so frequently happened, were bound to get mixed up in any excitement that came along, often to their own honor and glory.

There, the rocket had burst, and yet so quickly had Tubby grasped the situation, being considerably worked up at the time, that he had arrived at a conclusion before this took place.

He plainly saw the fiery stars scatter, and imagined he could even detect the faint boom of the rocket's bursting in midair, though Tubby would never affirm this fact positively.

Now they were moving on again, as before, every fellow feeling as he went, and hoping to be the lucky one whose itching fingers might come in contact with the wire. How this was to be severed when found, Tubby did not know, but he was willing to leave all that to Rob. Why, so well prepared did the scout master usually go that Tubby more than half believed he must be carrying with him a little pair of wire-cutters—at least he had a hazy remembrance of having once seen a minute sample of such a useful tool among Rob's traps. Even though this did not turn out to be so, trust him for making a good use of his knife, with its largest blade in condition to do the ripping and sawing of the small insulated copper wire; why, Tubby himself had many a time bent and twisted such a delicate strand, yes, and parted it, without any sort of tool, when he was fixing the electric doorbell at home, or making and arranging a bell connection so that his mother could summon the servant from the kitchen by pressing her toe upon a button concealed under the rug and table of the dining-room.

How beautiful this blind confidence on the part of Tubby! It is ever a delight to have a chum upon whom you can always fully depend when the storm clouds gather and danger presses around! Rob had ever been such a stanch rock to his comrades in times past. They had reason to throw their troubles on his shoulders without scruple.

Perhaps only two or three minutes had gone by since first they discovered that the enemy was concealed near by, yet the time seemed much longer than that to the anxious hearts of the wire searchers. Donald was listening with all his might. He dreaded lest he catch the sound of an approaching train while their important errand was still unfinished; and thinking thus he burned with undiminished zeal as he went groping amidst the small weeds that covered the ground over which they were crawling.

Indeed, Donald was not alone in his ambition to accomplish

something, for Rob and Andy themselves would have called it the happiest event of their lives could they have made the discovery for which every one yearned.

By now they had reached a point far enough away from the danger zone to permit with safety of a hurried consultation between Rob and Donald, provided it was carried on with the utmost discretion, each in turn placing his lips close to the ear of the other. Rob had ceased creeping. At first those behind hoped he had found what they were looking for, but in this they were soon undeceived, for they saw him putting his head against that of the Canadian boy and could just manage to catch a breath of the sibilant whispered conference that began.

It was at this very moment that a slant of the light breeze brought the rumble of the oncoming heavy freight train to their ears. To the imaginative Tubby it seemed as though it must proceed from a spot only a mile or so distant. With that elusive wire still unfound the prospect did not look very encouraging, Tubby was bound to admit, though still trying to bolster up his courage.

CHAPTER XX
THE MUNITION TRAIN'S APPROACH

"Do ye not hear it comin', Rab?" Donald asked in the other's ear. "Something must be done, or it will be too late!"

"We will find the wire, Donald," the scout master assured him.

"Oh! ay, but will it be in time?" begged the other.

Rob understood what doubts and fears were racking that faithful heart. He also had a plan whereby Donald might make assurance doubly certain. The time had apparently arrived when a division of their forces would appear to be the best policy.

"Listen, Donald," said Rob, still in that low whisper that even the other fellows could not catch, though they tried very hard to do so, "you must climb the bank, and, perhaps, find one of the guards. Failing that, you can run back along the track so as to warn your father of the danger. You know how to do that, and here is my little torch you might use, also some matches, my red bandanna to put over the light as a danger signal, and a part of a newspaper. Do you get my meaning clearly, Donald?"

"Oh! ay," said the eager boy, as he clutched all that Rob was thrusting into his hand. "Shall I go the noo, Rab?"

"Yes, be off with you," came the command. "Be careful how you stand up when you reach the top of the embankment. The enemy are hiding down here, and would outline you against the sky. Crawl all you can, Donald. Good-bye, and good luck go with you. Meanwhile, depend on us to find that wire!"

A fervent clasp of the hand. Donald crept hastily away, heading so as to reach the bank at the terminus of the trestle; for, of course, he could not hope to climb the latter itself.

Andy was able to partly guess what mission Rob had given into the keeping of the young Canadian. Possibly Andy would have liked being sent forth on such an exciting errand himself, but then he recognized the fact that Donald really had a superior claim to such a task. He was at home on his native heath, and could better make the Canadian guards understand, if he had the good luck to come upon any of those in whose care the bridge had been placed by the authorities. Then, again, it was his father whose life was in danger. Another thing satisfied Andy that Rob knew what was best in selecting Donald for action—being brought up in a railroading family he was apt to be much better acquainted with the ways by which signals are given calculated to stop trains. Yes, Donald was the proper one to be chosen, Andy concluded, and, as usual, Rob had wisely placed "a round peg in a round hole."

After their force had been diminished, the rest of the party continued their hunt for the hidden wire. Rob knew just about how it would be staked down as close to the earth as possible, by means of metal staples, or wickets like those used in the game of croquet, only much more diminutive. This would be done in order to prevent any passer-by from catching his foot in the wire, and thus bringing about an astonishing discovery that would break up all the plans of the plotters.

So Rob was feeling very carefully. He did not mean to miss anything while engaging in the search. He was also positive that they ought to run across the wire at any second.

But once more the breeze brought the sound of the approaching train more plainly to their ears. It was coming fast, they understood. In imagination Tubby could see the glare of the headlight in the west, though a second look convinced him he was probably mistaken, and that it was only one of the largest planets about setting below the horizon. After that he breathed freely again.

If Donald were only successful in meeting one of the guards, and could explain matters in a great hurry, a man might be sent down the track to wave a red lantern and thus stop the oncoming train. Failing in that, Donald must do the best he could with what Rob had provided for the purpose.

But even though this were done, the costly and invaluable bridge would not be saved unless that necessary wire were quickly discovered. Rob himself was beginning to feel a little worried over the matter. He thought they should have come upon it before then, unless his calculations were all awry. At the same time this did not mean he was ready to quit and call the game off, for that was hardly his way of doing things. They took more desperate chances with every foot that they drew nearer the threatened trestle, for it was impossible to say how far some of the timbers might be hurled when the explosion came, if it eventually did. That would depend altogether on the amount and concentrated energy of the explosive used; those men undoubtedly meant to do the most damage they could while about it.

Rob, in the start, could easily have covered three times as much ground as he did, and also discovered what he was looking for, had he dared use that wonderful little torch of his, which he had given to Donald. But this would have been utterly out of the question. It must have excited the suspicions of the concealed invaders, and caused them to hasten the culmination of their plans; or even, failing that, the attention of the armed guards above must have been attracted to the spot; and they were under orders to send a volley *first* at any moving object, and investigate afterward.

Foot by foot they continued to thoroughly comb every bit of territory over which they crept. If Rob failed to happen on the wire possibly Andy, or Zeb, or even Tubby might be the lucky one. They knew enough to understand that such a discovery was to be instantly communicated to the leader, so that he might start trying to sever communications.

Rob managed to cast frequent glances up toward the spot where he knew the solid ground was banked by a concrete wall, and the heavy beams of the trestle began. He wondered whether Donald would be as careful as he had cautioned him about showing himself, or if the boy, in his eagerness to save his father, would betray his presence by standing upright when on the embankment. So Rob was kept in a nervous state. Once he felt sure he heard a small stone rolling down the bank, possibly dislodged by the foot of the climber. He hoped that its descent had not been noticed by those men waiting in the clump of bushes toward the south; or that a vigilant member of the bridge guard would not come hurrying to the spot, ready to blaze away down the slope.

Andy had advanced a little after Donald's departure. He was now almost alongside his chum and leader, ready to receive any necessary communication that Rob would think fit to pass along. Apparently the other saw no necessity for any exchange of opinions. He said not a word as he went on, foot by foot, feeling the dead grass, and the weeds that grew in profusion along the lower level close to the river's verge, always hoping that the next movement would bring success.

It was Andy clutching his coat that caused Rob to look sideways, for the chum chanced to be on his left. This caused him to see what evidently Andy had reference to. Another rocket was swiftly climbing upward into the heavens; he could follow its yellow flight by the line of fire that trailed behind.

Even as he looked it described a beautiful turn and started earthward again, only to suddenly burst and discharge a swarm of writhing serpents that went wriggling this way and that until they disappeared from view.

Plainly, then, a second confederate of the plotters, on duty at another station still closer to the bridge, was endeavoring to let them know the doomed munition train was passing there, and was on its way eastward. The change from stars to serpents was significant in the eyes of Rob. But after all what did it matter, when they already knew that much? The sound of the heavy train reached them continuously, now rising higher, and anon falling to a lower pitch, but constantly in evidence.

The lay of the land compelled a closer approach to the embankment as they advanced, though Rob would much rather have kept a fair distance away, taking as little chance of danger as he consistently could. He did not yet give up hope of succeeding in his mission. At any second they were likely to discover what they sought.

Rob had it all planned out, how to cut the wire and balk the game those sneaking plotters had arranged. Perhaps he even gripped his wire-cutters in his hand, or at least knew where he could clutch them instantly when needed.

It was at this interesting time Rob felt certain he saw a dim object roll over the top of the embankment, much as a dog might do on occasion. Unless one were intently observing the particular spot where this took place the scout master did not believe Donald's action would be noticed.

The Canadian lad had gained the goal of his hopes, and if the spirit moved him he was in a position to hurry along the up-track, so as to meet the train. Rob wished he would do this. He was sorry now he had not embodied this in his orders to Donald, instead of leaving it to his discretion. If he started to look for one of the bridge guards he was apt to waste valuable time. He also ran a great risk of being fired upon before being able to explain who he was, and tell about the amazing thing that had brought him there in the darkness of night.

Still, Rob rather fancied that this would be Donald's plan. The great affection he bore for his father would overcome all his scruples while he climbed the bank. Rob had actually left it all to his discretion, and love would bias him along the line of least resistance. Yes, Rob believed more and more now that this was what Donald would conclude to be his duty. It gave the scout leader considerable satisfaction to think so.

After the danger was past, with the munition train halted before it reached the beginning of the trestle and the mine prevented from being discharged by the wire being cut in two —that would be time enough to explain things to the guard, running toward the stalled engine to find out what had happened to cause the sudden stop.

If all worked well, victory would be in their grasp pretty soon now; but, oh, Tubby found himself oppressed with a dreadful fear that there might come a hitch in the beautiful program, which would mean a disastrous end to all their hopes.

Was there a wire at all, he asked himself? Could it be possible for those clever German sympathizers to make use of some cunning method for discharging the mine by means of wireless? All sorts of wonderful things were cropping up every day Over There where nations were engaged in the death grapple. Who could say what might not be accomplished? Tubby remembered reading how a Yankee had proved that he could control a torpedo spinning through the water by electrical appliances similar to wireless, so that he could send it to the right or to the left as he willed and cause it to hunt after an object a mile or more distant, just as a magnet is attracted toward the North Star by some mysterious unseen power. Tubby was in a condition to believe anything, no matter how amazing.

Then the fat scout noted that once more Rob—yes, and Andy, too—had stopped short. They appeared to be examining something on the ground, and Tubby's heart commenced to thump like mad as he speculated upon what this meant. Was it the wire they had been so industriously hunting all this while? Oh, he would willingly give all he possessed in the way of boyish treasures, could he only be assured of this and know that Rob had severed the same.

Tubby heaved a sigh of genuine relief. He had heard a low chirp, peculiar in itself and yet not at all calculated to arouse any suspicion. It was the most welcome sound that could have reached the hearing of the anxious, nerve-racked Tubby. By it he became aware that success had indeed rewarded their patient efforts. The copper wire was located at last!

CHAPTER XXI
CUTTING THE BATTERY CONNECTIONS

That was what had happened. Rob turned out to be the lucky one. Andy might have run upon the wire a couple of seconds later, for his hand was at the time groping near that of his chum.

The wire was held down close to the ground by frequent metal wickets, as Rob had figured might be the case, for that would have been his own method of concealing the wire, and could be easily accomplished by a second man who crept after the one allowing the wire to free itself from the big spool he carried.

Rob was not bothering himself about these details now. To get that wire cut in twain before the man handling the battery at the other end sent the electric current along that would discharge the mine—that was his one endeavor.

Tubby knew he was working to accomplish this end. He watched what was going on so close by, though Rob and Andy could only be seen indistinctly; but Tubby was able to easily supply through a lively imagination whatever was lacking.

Tubby turned his head and looked toward the span. In imagination he could see it give a sudden, terrible heave and go flying in many fragments toward the sky!

Just when it was beginning to get unbearable, so that Tubby was almost forced to shout out, the suspense ended. He knew from the chuckle that Andy could not for the life of him suppress, that the wire had yielded to the force Rob was applying, and no longer ran in a connected line from mine to battery!

As long as he lived Tubby would surely never, never forget the spasm of glorious feeling that shot through his whole mind and body when he realized this stupendous fact. When one has been straining might and main to accomplish a given thing, and at the last gasp victory comes into his hand, that is the time he feels like a world conqueror and would not change places with any king living. Tubby passed through this experience, even though his may not have been the hand to wield those magical little pliers with which the wire had been severed. However, the honor and glory was great enough to go all around, and every fellow who had anything to do with the deed ought to share in the result.

Rob, having cut the wire, hastened to wind one end about the nearest stout bush he could reach, choosing the base, so as to have it afford effectual resistance.

This was that portion of the broken wire which had connection with the battery; the other end he cared nothing about, since the mine had been rendered harmless. It was just as well that the plotters did not know in too big a hurry how their cunning scheme had been nipped in the bud. Time enough for that when the fellow finally pressed his battery key into service, only to find to his utter amazement and disgust that no roaring response followed his action.

"Well," Tubby gloatingly told himself, "perhaps those chaps would be a surprised lot when they found out what a mess they had made of it, not only missing the destruction of the million-dollar munition train, but failing to even blow up the bridge itself as intended. There's many a slip between the cup and the lip, they say. I guess it was a bad hour for your schemes, my boys, when Rob Blake put his foot in this affair. As usual, it promises to wind up in fresh glory for the Eagles."

Tubby was not the only one who breathed more freely after the wire was cut. Rob and Andy, possibly also Zeb, felt like chuckling as the culminating stroke was given that put it out of the power of the men hidden in the bushes to carry out their dark designs.

Rob suddenly became more ambitious. Why be satisfied with half a job, when still more could be accomplished? What was to hinder them from getting help from the guards who watched over the railway property at this particular point— soldiers in uniform, undoubtedly—and trying to effect the capture of the unseen miscreants who had dishonored the hospitality afforded by Uncle Sam?

Rob had hardly given this thought any attention up to now, but once it gripped him he allowed it to have full sway. But nothing could be done until the train either stopped short or else proceeded across the bridge. He believed the former was certain to be the case, for Donald, not being sure the danger was abated, would never let his father speed past and enter upon the danger zone.

"She's coming fast now," breathed Andy in the other's ear. "There, that whistle must be meant as a signal to those at the bridge. All trains do that before getting too close, so the engineer can be given a right-of-way signal."

Rob somehow did not try to stop Andy from saying this. In fact, he was not feeling one half so solicitous over the risk of being heard by the plotters, as before he had rendered their cause hopeless. About this time he noticed that there was a strange grinding noise in connection with the rumble of the near-by train. He understood from this that brakes were being hurriedly applied.

They could now see the glare of the headlight. Apparently the train had shot out from some cut where the banks up to that moment had concealed its presence.

This would indicate, Rob believed, that some one must have signalled to the man in the cab to pull up; in such troublous times the engineer had to quickly obey such a summons, especially when approaching this bridge, which was known to be the most dangerous point along the entire line, since it was so vulnerable to an attack from raiders.

Rob could also easily believe that Donald himself was responsible for the waving of the red light that spelled danger. He must have made up his mind while climbing the bank that he could afford to take no chances, and that saving the train, as well as his father, was his most pressing duty.

Well, no one could blame the boy, for in so doing he only obeyed the dictates of his loyal heart. As has been already stated, Rob would have told him to carry out this very thing if it had occurred to him forcibly at the time they parted company.

The quartette crouching on the low ground not a great way from the trestle now heard loud voices. The guards were running forward, some of them, to find out the reason of the train stopping as it did when they had given no signal. Possibly it might be some clever trick of an enemy lurking near by, to draw them away from the bridge, so that damage of some sort could be attempted; and hence being cautious as well as brave they divided their force, a portion remaining spread along the structure in order to shoot down any loiterer who could not answer their challenge properly.

"Rob, why don't we make a move?" pleaded Andy, unable to check his customary impatience.

"Hold your horses," the scout master told him. "We ought to wait until Donald has had a fair chance to explain. Then the soldiers can learn about our being down here and will not fire on us if we commence to climb the bank. Only for that, they might let loose; and it's a mighty poor time to apologize to a fellow after he's dead. Tubby?"

"Yes, Rob, what is it?" came softly from nearby.

"What are you doing?"

"Why, don't you know, Rob, I've just been holding my finger on the pulse of those men who have made such a bad mess of their brilliant plan; and, honest to goodness, Rob, I believe they know by this time that they've been hoodwinked, kerflummixed, and also knocked silly."

"But how do you know all that, Tubby?" gasped the astonished Andy.

"Oh, I've been feeling the wire, you see. It gave several of the most vicious pulls ever, just like the chap at the battery end couldn't understand why no explosion came along when he pressed the button and turned on the juice, so to speak. It is to laugh, fellows. This looks like a second Waterloo, only it's the German neutrality-breakers who are up against it this time, instead of the heroic French."

Now, both of the others considered that this was quite a clever piece of strategy, and particularly for a boy like Tubby, whose wits would so often go wool-gathering, instead of netting prompt returns. Indeed, Andy felt chagrined to think that it had never once occurred to him to try this scheme. Tubby had scored heavily, for once. He was evidently quite proud of his success, too, for they could hear an occasional queer chuckle emanating from the place where he had squatted down like an enormous toad, ready to stay or go, as Rob decided.

The running guards were drawing near the stalled engine which continued to pant and throb as locomotives do when under a full head of steam and standing still on the rails. The soldiers would be quickly put in possession of the main facts by Donald, who would be vouched for by his father.

Rob turned and looked in the direction where, as he fully believed, the unknown invaders from the other side of the boundary line had been recently secreted. He wondered what they were doing, now that they realized how their game was up, and that unless they succeeded in taking themselves off in a hurry they might yet be made victims of the rifles of the Canadian bridge guards.

By this time Donald must have told the astounded guards enough of the story to cause them to refrain from using their ready guns when dark figures were seen coming up the bank. Yes, there was Donald calling out to them, saying the coast was clear and that it was all right for his four friends to come up so as to corroborate his amazing story.

CHAPTER XXII
LIKE OLD TIMES FOR THE SCOUTS

"There, that settles it. Donald wants us to show up," Tubby broke out with, rejoiced in the opportunity to discontinue his long silence.

"Are we going, Rob?" demanded Andy, even more impatient.

"Come along, everybody!" decided the scout master.

With that they arose to their feet, the distressing period of crouching and trying to hide themselves being at an end. They could all take deep breaths and begin to experience some of the joy that comes with the advent of victory after a hard-fought battle.

Rob led the way, and they quickly arrived at the foot of the steep embankment which marked the joining of the railway with the beginning of the trestle. Up this they started bravely. Tubby began to have his own troubles immediately, for, as might be expected, the soil started to crumble more or less under his feet. Tubby was unusually awkward about getting a footing.

Several times he started to slide back, and only recovered himself with difficulty. Then came an occasion when he failed to secure a grip, and as his weight caused the earth and stones to crumble more and more under him Tubby commenced rolling down the slope like a barrel, clawing at a wild rate to the right and to the left.

He undoubtedly would have gone all of the route and brought up where he began his climb, much the worse for his experience, but for Zeb. The big Maine guide chanced to be below the rest, and was thus able to reach out and seize upon the revolving Tubby. By bracing himself, Zeb also managed to bring the other to a full stop. Tubby was in luck, as usually happened. He once again started upward, as if he were the famous youth in the poem whose motto, when climbing the snow-clad heights, was "Excelsior"; only Tubby did not expect to meet with the other's sad fate.

In this fashion, assisted by the man of the woods, Tubby was enabled to finally gain the top of the embankment. Rob and Andy had already advanced to join the little group of excited men hurrying toward the spot.

There was Donald in the lead, with a sturdy man in overalls at his side, whose arm was proudly thrown across the boy's shoulders; for Robert McGuffey realized that his boy had covered the family name with honor by his action. Then came the conductor of the train, a man in uniform, who carried a lighted lantern, together with a number of soldiers armed with guns. Every one of them seemed eager and full of enthusiasm, for the war no longer lay thousands of miles off, with an ocean rolling between—it had actually come to their very doors.

One man, who Rob could see was an officer, he thought a lieutenant at least, immediately bustled up and faced him. He leaned forward and looked earnestly into the face of the scout, whose khaki uniform must have interested him.

"This boy who turns out to be the engineer's son," he hurriedly said, "tells us you and your comrades are American lads and that you have crossed the boundary to give warning that a vile plot was on foot to dynamite the bridge. Is this the truth, or a fairy story?"

"Yes, it is what brings us here, sir," replied Rob simply. "Most of the credit for discovering the truth belongs to Donald McGuffey."

"No, no; for where would I have been only for your finding me caught in the auld bear trap?" cried the other energetically. "Besides, I never could hae reached here alone, in time to save the bridge. If there be any honor, every one o' ye shares in the same."

"This sounds very fine," said the officer, who could hardly bring himself to believe that it was the truth. "What proof have you to back your story up?"

Impulsive Andy could contain himself no longer. He was more than a little indignant that their word should be even doubted.

"Rob, show them, won't you? Seeing is believing every time,

and we've got all the proof any one would want, a dozen times over."

"Yes, show him, Rob, please do!" urged Tubby, also beginning to feel a righteous indignation.

"If you will come with us, sir," Rob told the officer, "you can see enough to convince you we have told nothing but the truth."

"Lead on, and we will follow," the other commanded; and then, turning, he added something in low tones to a couple of his men, who immediately closed in on either side of the boys and Zeb.

But Rob only smiled. He could easily afford to laugh, knowing as he did what was in store for the Doubting Thomas of a Canadian officer, who, fearful of being made the victim of a joke, would not believe without positive evidence.

Accordingly down the bank they all plunged, while the engine continued to fret near by, as though repenting of having been stopped short. Possibly Tubby would have excelled all the rest in making that descent, for he had already commenced to slide, and in another moment must have taken a header, only for the strong arm of Zeb, the Maine guide, having hovered near in the rôle of protector and defender.

Once at the bottom, Rob, taking in his bearings, led the way directly to the spot where, with his comrades, he had been lately crouching. The first thing he did on arriving was to take the lighted lantern from the hand of the train conductor and hold it close to the ground.

"There is the copper insulated wire that ran from the battery to the planted mine," he explained.

The officer, bending forward, looked it over. His doubts began to vanish, for surely this seemed like stern business.

"Who cut this wire?" he demanded sharply.

"I did, sir," replied Rob modestly.

"What was your object in doing it?" continued the soldier, eyeing the scout with kindling interest.

"We knew that the first thing to be done was to prevent those conspirators from using their battery to discharge the mine," explained Rob, "and that if only we could come upon the connections and sever them they would have their teeth drawn. But it was only at the last minute we managed to find the concealed wire; for as you can see, sir, they had it pinned close to the ground with these metal staples."

He pulled one of the crooked bits of stout wire up as he spoke and showed them how craftily it worked. Everybody pushed forward to see. The conductor of the million-dollar freight knew he was losing valuable time and would have to run additionally fast if he ever hoped to make it up; but the story of the scout interested him deeply, and, besides, it had a direct bearing on the safety of himself and crew, so he felt justified in lingering.

"Now," continued Rob, "none of us has as yet set eyes on any mine. We only believe one has been planted under the trestle here. It would be the right thing for us to follow up this broken wire and see for ourselves how true this theory is. Shall we start, sir?"

"Without a second's delay!" snapped the aroused lieutenant. "There may yet be sufficient time to pursue the rascals and bring them to justice for this attempted outrage. And believe me, boy, we will make them pay dearly for their fun, if only we can lay hands on the cowardly curs!"

Still holding the lantern, and followed by the group, Rob was already tracing the course of the pinned-down copper wire. As he had the conductor's light, of course that worthy had to keep trotting at his heels, which was sufficient excuse for further delay on his part.

They speedily came to the high trestle, and passed under the heavy beams and timbers of which it was constructed. Then there were exclamations that ran the whole gamut of wonder and horror, when the end of the wire showed them a small box that contained enough explosives to wreck the entire structure, for it had been artfully placed so as to do the utmost damage possible.

"Lift up that box and handle it carefully, two of you men," ordered the officer. "Soak it in the river, and stand guard over it until relieved. We will want it as evidence when handing in a report of this mad adventure."

Hardly waiting to see that they started to carry out his instructions, he turned once more upon Rob. Now there was only admiration in the officer's manner of speaking to the boy.

"We apparently owe a great deal to the efficiency of you and your brave scout comrades, my lad," said the now convinced lieutenant. "Perhaps you could add still further to the debt by showing us where those scoundrels were in hiding, waiting to fire the mine. I confess an overpowering desire to follow them, and save them the trouble of recrossing the boundary line."

"Nothing easier, sir," calmly replied Rob. "All we have to do is to follow the other half of the broken wire and it will lead us to their nest."

"Well, I should say so!" chuckled Andy, wondering why the officer had not hit upon this very simple method instantly; but then, Andy reflected, the poor fellow had in his youth never had the chance of becoming a scout and learning the art of using his wits to look for the cause of things, as well as cultivating the habit of observation.

Back they hurried in an eager bunch to the spot where Rob had severed the connecting link with his little combination pliers and wire-cutter. Here the other line was taken up. It led them toward the identical spot where the boys had previously decided the plotting invaders were hidden. This proved to be a clump of dense bushes, affording an excellent refuge secure from discovery, although it was near enough to the railway embankment to allow observation.

"You see, here's the battery," laughed Rob, making good use of the lantern again, and everybody gasped as they saw what he was pointing at.

Everybody gasped as they saw what he was pointing at.

Apparently, when the men in hiding had failed to fire the mine and realized that their terrible plot had "missed connections" in some strange way, they must have been suddenly overwhelmed with a panic, for they had fled in such haste that no attempt had been made to carry off their belongings, and so the fine little battery was abandoned to its fate.

There was no longer the shadow of a doubt in the mind of the wary lieutenant. He forgot that he had mistrusted these boys in the beginning, and suspected that they were trying to gain some glory, without any real basis for their wonderful story. All this Rob understood when the other impulsively grasped and squeezed his hand, at the same time exclaiming:

"I am proud to meet you, my brave young chap. I only regret

that you are not a Canadian like Donald here. You have done us a tremendous favor by your energy and your Yankee smartness. I am going to ask you to help us still further. If only we could capture those villains, it would complete this wonderful night's work. Will you accompany me with several of my men, while we try and cut them off before they can recross the line and find refuge in the States?"

"Oh, Rob!" cried Andy; and that was all he said, but there was a world of entreaty in those two words.

The scout master, whose indignation had been fully aroused because of that late near-tragedy, in which his country would have been undoubtedly involved, did not take ten seconds to make up his mind.

"Yes, we'll gladly coöperate with you to try and round them up, sir; three of us at least will go with you, and the sooner we start the better chances we'll have for success."

CHAPTER XXIII
IN SWIFT PURSUIT

Tubby grunted.

He immediately understood that Rob did not mean to include *him* in the party that was to try and cut the invaders off before they could recross the boundary line. Really, Tubby did not know whether to be glad or sorry. To be sure, he always wanted to have a hand in everything patriotic that was going on, which might reflect credit on the scout uniform; and in one way he would have dearly delighted in being present, should those unknown plotters be brought to book. But then it promised to prove an arduous undertaking, since all possible haste must be made; and this would necessitate driving through the brush with utter disregard as to who was tagging along at the rear of the procession, a place Tubby occupied about ten times out of ten.

Well, to be philosophical, Tubby concluded to calmly abide by whatever decision Rob arrived at. As scout leader he ought to know what was best for all concerned, and really it would be much more comfortable sitting there with the bridge guards and chatting, rather than butting up against unseen trees and getting "the map of Ireland" scratched on his face by a score of thorny bushes.

The train conductor could not think of accompanying them, though he generously told Rob to keep the lantern; this trifling sacrifice was the least thing he could do to show his deep gratitude, for it looked as though his life might have paid the penalty, only for the valor of these three scouts and Donald.

The engineer had to return with him, too, and there was an affectionate parting between Mr. McGuffey and his boy; for, despite his lame leg, Donald—that stubborn Scotch blood showing again—had concluded that he, too, wanted to be in the chase.

So Rob, Andy, Zeb and Donald, together with the lieutenant and two of his men, started off in hot haste. Too many precious minutes had already been taken up with this hunt for the hidden mine; the panic-stricken fugitives by now must be well on their way toward the border, and unless the pursuers were smart they would never overtake them in time.

One thing was in their favor: The men from the other side could not be very well acquainted with the locality. They had been able to reach the vicinity of the trestle and the bridge which they had doomed for destruction by making use of the map drawn and the aerial photographs taken by the pilot of the aeroplane, that had hovered over the railway embankment on that occasion witnessed by the scouts; but now that this near-panic had gripped them, there was a chance of becoming twisted in their bearings and losing their way.

Tubby went back to the bridge, and, making friends with several young fellows, he quickly won a way to their regard by his chummy manner. Tubby never lacked for friends because his warm heart quickly aroused a feeling of reciprocation. He was soon seated, with a number of deeply interested fellows in uniform, telling of the amazing things he, Rob and Merritt Crawford had seen—yes, and been engaged in also—when across the water in the fighting zones of Belgium and France. As none of these sturdy sons of Canada had as yet crossed, and they were all deeply interested in everything connected with the ferocious warfare going on over the sea, it can be readily understood that Tubby soon lost his humorous aspect in their eyes, induced by his rotund figure, and became a genuine hero.

Meanwhile the train had once more started, crossing the bridge in safety, thanks to the work of Rob and his chums. It was soon miles away from the danger point, heading toward the blue sea, to have its million-dollar cargo stowed in the holds of various steamers bound for the direction of the fighting fronts.

Since Rob had elected to accompany the hunting party, it must be our duty to keep track of the doings of this detachment. Donald and Zeb were called upon once more to exercise their judgment with regard to reaching the border by the shortest possible route. This would be the very path over which they had come; and in a short time Rob, upon using the lantern, decided that the fugitives had made use of another route, for there was no sign of tracks heading south. He could easily pick out their own footprints, especially those plain ones made by Tubby; but in no instance were they superseded by fresher tracks.

This did not discourage them in the least. In fact, Donald declared he felt sure he knew how the fugitives would go, as there was only a choice between two trails, unless they lost themselves and wandered aimlessly to and fro.

Somewhere close to the border he declared it would be possible for them to make a swift turn and cut across to the other trail, upon hearing which the officer displayed considerable satisfaction.

"That sounds well to me, Donald," he told the engineer's son. "Put us where we can lie in ambush and surprise those fiends, and you will be doing your country the greatest possible service. I would willingly give five years of my own life for an opportunity to take those rascals and show the curs who plot to ruin our cause what it means to invade Canada from a friendly country."

Rob, in a measure, could feel for the officer. His own indignation had kept growing the more he considered what the probable result of an explosion must have been, with that train on the trestle at the time. Yes, while scouts were not supposed to take sides with either party in the great war being waged—and Rob had shown on several notable occasions that he had a warm feeling for the German people, much as he hated the methods by means of which their leaders were conducting the campaign of frightfulness—at the same time he considered that these plotters had by their action placed themselves outside the pale of scout law. Rob looked upon them not as heroes daring deadly perils for the sake of their beloved Fatherland, but in the light of cowardly schemers who would creep up and do a terrible crime without taking any great risk themselves.

As haste was the chief object now, everything else had to give way to this one thing. It was entirely different from their former advance along this trail—when they did not know what dangers lurked about them and were compelled to move along in the semi-darkness, almost groping their way at times. Now with that lantern showing them all obstacles they made rapid progress. Besides, it almost seemed to Rob as though he were familiar with the route.

Then again a little later Rob came around to look at things in still another light. He was not inclined to be bloodthirsty, as a rule, and since the great plot had failed, perhaps it might be just as well if the men escaped. They could spread the disastrous story among their kind in the States, and thus discourage any renewal of similar activities.

They were making good time. Even Donald, limping along, managed to keep his proud position as leader of the expedition. The praise that had come his way of late, from his own father as well as others, had acted like a bracing tonic upon his entire system, and encouraged him to make further drafts upon his physical strength.

Andy, leaving all the labor of following the path to those in the lead, devoted himself to keeping a wary eye upon the surrounding forest. He cherished a faint hope that possibly the fugitives, having become lost, might think to go into camp; and if they were incautious enough to start a fire Andy wanted to be the one to spy it out first.

Nothing happened up to the time when they glimpsed that rocky cairn which marks the dividing line between Canada and the United States.

"Here is the border, sir," said Donald to the lieutenant, "and ye ken the ither trail lies yonder toward the east. If so be we gang awa' ower that way it is probable that we may run across the wretches."

"Then let us start without any more delay, Donald," decided the officer.

"Do you think, Donald," ventured Rob, "that you can take us there without the use of this lantern? If we keep on as we are going, I'm afraid they will glimpse the light and give us the slip. How about it, Donald?"

"Oh, ay, it will nae be so verra hard, I ween," instantly replied the confident young Canadian, as the scout master anticipated he would. So the light was "doused," and they continued their forward movement with only the stars to afford any illumination.

They turned abruptly to the left, and headed into the east. Donald assured them that about this point the other trail did not lie more than two-thirds of a mile away; and he felt pretty positive they would be able to make it before the fugitives, stumbling along in the half-darkness, could get there.

At first they found it rather difficult walking, for their eyes had become accustomed to the assistance given by the train conductor's splendid lantern, and there were more or less frequent collisions with trees and stumps and unseen rocks. But by degrees this difficulty was removed, and the accidents became less numerous.

Andy was once more feeling that prickly sensation commencing to chase along his spine, such as approaching excitement always engendered. Andy was not thinking along the same lines as Rob. He really *yearned* to see the rascals pay the penalty. Andy would not have been at all concerned could he see them fall into the hands of the military authorities of Canada, even knowing that in times of war they must be taken before a court-martial and in all probability would be condemned to be summarily shot by a firing squad.

Once again Andy was using his eyes in the endeavor to make some sort of pleasing discovery. He wanted to shine more in the limelight; thus far circumstances had not been kind to him, for he had not been permitted to take a leading part in anything that had occurred; and Andy was ambitious.

They had been moving on for some time without anything happening, when he suddenly had a distinct thrill. What could that faint glow mean that he had just discovered ahead? It was true that it lay somewhat to the right, and Andy imagined this might mean American territory instead of that belonging to Canada; but then who would know the difference, and if the prisoners were carried back to the railway there would never be any proof that they had been taken on foreign soil.

Andy had a brief struggle in his mind over this, and then he decided that under the circumstances it would be easily justifiable; at any rate, far be it from him to venture to call the circumstance to the attention of the officer in charge of the pursuit. If the lieutenant chose to take it upon himself to consider that they were still north of the line, why, so it must go on the records.

Having salved his conscience in this rather elastic fashion, which was quite wrong in a scout, though Andy would not allow himself to believe it, the boy concluded to direct the attention of his companions to the glow as soon as he detected it again.

This happened a minute or so later, and Andy, having figured out his course, hastened to remark eagerly:

"Rob, look over there to the right, will you? That must mean a camp fire is burning back of some mound or clump of thick brush, wouldn't you think?"

Every one looked. It was evidently the consensus of opinion, to judge from the various remarks that arose, that Andy was correct. Undoubtedly a small fire was burning in that quarter, and what more likely than that the fugitives, believing themselves safe across the border, had decided to halt and repair such damages as they may have suffered during their mad flight through the dark woods?

CHAPTER XXIV
THOSE WHO SAT BY THE FIRE

"They must have made better time than we gave them credit for," Andy went on to say, in his conclusive fashion, as though there could be no doubt about the matter. "But," he continued, with a queer chuckle, "after all, they've been silly enough to stop short and go into camp. Now's our chance to give 'em the greatest surprise going."

Apparently Andy had convinced himself that the fire was on the Canadian side of the line. Since it was more or less of a mythical division, how were they to know the exact point of separation? Besides, those scheming men, who never once regarded the sacrifice of human life as worth weighing in the balance, when trying to strike at Great Britain in such a cowardly way, deserved little, if any, consideration.

If any doubt existed in Rob's mind regarding the situation he said nothing about it. With that lieutenant present Rob felt in no way responsible for affairs. He, too, was under orders now, and the success or failure of the plan of campaign rested wholly on the young officer's shoulders.

"We will try to surprise them," remarked the other; "and no time should be lost in going about it. If you three boys will keep alongside me as we advance, we can arrange a plan, for I shall certainly be glad of your efficient help."

Rob thought that was nicely put. It looked as though the military defender of the bridge had indeed radically altered the first opinion he entertained in connection with the scouts. Well, Rob Blake was the last fellow in the wide world to bear any animosity toward another on account of first impressions, which he knew only too well were often wrong.

Accordingly they made a start, but a warning was also issued begging every one to be extra careful how he stumbled, lest the unwonted sound reach the ears of those by the fire, and as they would naturally be suspicious of every unusual noise, the consequences might be disastrous to their success.

When he came to discuss the merits of the situation with the lieutenant, and in turn was told what the other meant to do, Rob conceived a growing admiration for the young fellow. He really believed the other must have a most capable head on his shoulders; and it was also apparent to observing Rob that he showed positive signs of considerable military genius. In private life he may only have been a bank clerk in Montreal, or a Government employee in Ottawa; but after being called out in defense of his country he had plainly taken it upon himself to sink all else in the one overpowering fact that he was now a soldier, and must give up his whole mind to studying military tactics.

He really laid out quite a neat little plan of attack, whereby Zeb and the two soldiers could creep around to the other side of the fire so as to cut off any possible escape on the part of the fugitives brought to bay. Rob understood why the Maine guide had been selected in this manner; apparently the officer felt that Zeb would know just how to lead the two privates, so that they might manage to get around on the longer route without creating an alarm. He may himself have had experience with woods guides, and appreciated their accomplishments.

So Zeb and the two men went off. The others were to loiter a bit in order to give them a chance to cover the extra ground. A simple code of signals had also been arranged between the two parties, so that they could communicate with one another. In this fashion the officer had taken it upon himself to be in a position to order a general advance on both sides, when he thought the proper moment had come.

Rob heard all this, and his admiration increased. He was pleased to serve under such a smart head. Some upstarts, vested with a brief authority by the circumstance of war, would have strutted, and posed, and tried to show how consequential they could be; but this chap was of the right sort. Rob was willing to wager that he must come from good stock, and that some of his immediate ancestors had won their spurs on the field of Waterloo, or some place where British soldiers fought stubbornly and with bulldog courage against great odds.

As they advanced the fire began to be seen more frequently,

though the undulating nature of the intervening ground often caused it to remain concealed for a brief stretch of time. Andy and Rob, as well as Donald, were greatly interested in what they were about to see. They had had these plotters in their minds so much of late that naturally a most intense curiosity had been aroused concerning their identity.

Andy had invested them with almost supernatural powers and attributes. If all the thoughts that flitted through his active mind could be condensed into a concrete whole, those by the fire were apt to assume gigantic proportions indeed, and prove pretty dangerous customers for even half a dozen armed aggressors to attack.

But when Andy showed a disposition to hurry on faster than prudence would dictate, he was gently but firmly repressed by the lieutenant, a fact Rob noted with satisfaction.

They did not speak any more than was absolutely necessary, and then only in the softest of whispers. It was no time for comparing opinions, even Andy understood that much; consequently he was compelled to hold all his communications with himself.

Then there came the time when they began to detect moving figures about the fire, and this increased their interest. They could manage to make out just two men, one inclined to be tall, and as swarthy as an Indian, the other rather portly, though also of a generous size.

Well, so far as that went the boys had guessed before then that the number of those actually engaged in the work of trying to dynamite the railway span would turn out to be two, though they might have confederates scattered around the country, instructed to send them signals, it might be, or advise of any suspicious fact going to tell that the authorities were extra vigilant, as if having been warned that special danger menaced the bridge.

The closer they drew the more violently did Andy's heart pump. His excitement kept on growing by leaps and bounds. This, then, was to be the culmination of the remarkable adventure that had come to them so unsolicited during their visit to the woods of northern Maine. He wondered whether these two men were going to resist arrest, even when outnumbered three to one. That they were desperate characters went without saying, and they must know what their fate was likely to be, once the military authorities of Canada had them in their hands.

So Andy fingered his gun, and made up his mind how far he would be justified in using it under the conditions. As a scout, he had no business to seek glory such as a soldier would seek to attain; and yet there may be occasions when even a peace-loving scout, bound by the vows of his order, must display loyalty and courage, and be ready to defend the weak against a bully. He should also, Andy felt confident, be prompt to stand up for the laws of neutrality, and consider it his bounden duty to aid the authorities of a neighboring community to stop any bold raid that threatened to disrupt the peace.

Yes, it must be admitted that impulsive Andy was about ready to make stern use of his gun, if the occasion demanded such a necessity. He could aim so as to only wound the fellow at whom he fired; that was the extent his activity in the affair ought to reach, Andy decided, though for that matter, if the conspirators were bound to be set up before a firing squad anyhow they would be no worse off if they paid the full debt now.

The lieutenant interrupted his reflections, grim as they were becoming, nor was Andy sorry for it. Drawing their heads close together, the officer gave his last orders in the ears of his three followers. He had decided that they would stand a far better chance of advancing close in, without the risk of discovery, if they veered a little to the left, and then continued to creep up.

Rob saw that the scheme was a good one, for in that quarter lay a fringe of bushes that seemed dense enough to effectually conceal their movements. Once behind this barrier, they would feel more free to move as they pleased. It seemed that these accommodating bushes kept right on until only fifty feet away from the fire itself.

Really nothing better could have been devised. If he had had the management of the scheme in his own hands, Rob did not see how he could have improved upon the lieutenant's plan of action.

By now it was probable that Zeb and the two privates were nearing their post, having crept around the camp as ordered. In good time the signals arranged for could be exchanged, to make sure that all was ready; then the command to rise up and advance would be next in order—after that it depended on the state of desperation that would assail the fugitives whether any fighting must ensue, or the capture be carried out without bloodshed.

As the quartette of creepers drew near the terminus of the bush fringe they grew more and more cautious. By now they had reached a point so close to the fire that they plainly heard some one give vent to a laugh. This would seemingly indicate that while the plotters might be a desperate lot, at the same time their recent escapade had not entirely demoralized them. Andy felt a strange sensation creeping over him. He knew it could not be *fear*, because Andy always boasted that he had never experienced such a silly thing in all his life; and certainly there was no occasion for it now; indeed, the boot was on the other foot, and it should be these two trapped rascals who hovered near a condition of collapse after their recent narrow escape, and with peril still overshadowing them.

When Andy first peered out between the bushes he anticipated seeing a pair of desperadoes who, by their fierce appearance, would have shamed all the villains depicted on the screen at the movies. He had quite a shock when he discovered that nothing of the sort greeted his vision. In fact, had Andy happened on this camp by accident, knowing nothing about the bold raid across the border, he would never have suspected that two such dreadful villains could masquerade under such ordinary exteriors.

One of the men was tall and dark, with straight black hair, and a certain dignified way of doing his menial duties, for he was actually washing up a few tin dishes at the time—no, Andy corrected himself, for a second look told him these were of aluminum ware, the most expensive outfit any camper can purchase, and much preferable to any other on account of extreme lightness.

Well, at any rate, those terrible German sympathizers knew a good thing when they saw it, Andy decided. They had come prepared to stay out in the woods for days, if need be, until they received word, perhaps by aeroplane messenger, that an unusually heavy shipment of munitions had started east, and would arrive at a certain night in the neighborhood of the threatened bridge. Oh, it was very easy for clever Andy to figure all this out, and he secretly admired the way in which the two men had arranged things. They had prepared this camp beforehand, meaning to fly to its shelter after accomplishing the destruction of both bridge and train.

As to the second man, he puzzled Andy the most. The dark-faced member of the pair looked capable of any sort of crime, but that other chap certainly must be out of his element when engaging in such a dastardly act; for he laughed heartily and looked most genial as he sat there with his hands locked about his knees and watched the other handling the camp cooking outfit.

CHAPTER XXV
BAD LUCK, AND GOOD

Andy looked again and rubbed his eyes. It was certainly the most astonishing thing he could remember running across in all his experience, and only went to prove how deceptive appearances may be at times. But it gave him a shock to think that such a nice-looking old party, with a ring to his laugh, could underneath the outer veneer be such a desperate schemer as to want to blow up bridges and destroy trains and all such horrible things, just because he happened to have some German ancestors.

Really, Andy had already made up his mind that if he felt absolutely compelled to use his weapon at all he would confine his attentions to that swarthy chap, and leave the merry individual to others; for he felt positive that if he did anything to injure that jovial party he would never forgive himself. Which, under the circumstances, was exceedingly thoughtful and kind of Andy; and doubtless, if ever he ventured to confess as to what his magnanimous thoughts had been, he would find that his resolution was much appreciated.

Possibly Rob, too, was staring wonderingly at the occupants of that camp close to the border; for he must have been as much surprised as his chum at the unexpected mild appearance of the two desperadoes. Before he could find a chance to give vent to his feelings something came to pass that prevented their exchanging opinions.

Andy tugged at Rob's sleeve and whispered in an awed tone:

"Look there, will you, Rob; Zeb's got rattled, and he's bound to break up the whole bully scheme!"

They suddenly saw the lanky Maine guide standing up beyond the camp. He did not appear to care whether he was seen or not, judging from the boldness of his actions. It grew worse instead of better, for even while they looked what should Zeb do but start directly toward the fire!

At first Andy thought the other meant to attack the pair seated there, without waiting for any signal, which might be a piece of boldness on his part, but would also be disobeying the orders of the lieutenant. Then Andy had reason to stare some more and change his mind, for to his utter amazement Zeb trailed his rifle under his arm, when by rights a careful man would certainly have held it in such a position that it would be ready for quick work in case of necessity.

Would wonders never cease? Andy asked himself, as he continued to crouch there. First, there was the astonishing appearance of the chief villain, and now here was Zeb acting as though he had actually lost his head and meant to commit suicide.

Straight along came the woods guide. He looked solemn enough; indeed, Andy even thought Zeb had the appearance of a man who was up for sentence before a judge, and meant to throw himself on the mercy of the court.

Then Andy discovered that the dark-faced conspirator had discovered the coming of Zeb, which would indicate that he possessed pretty keen hearing. But how was this, that he did not instantly fly to where those two guns rested against the trunk of the pine near by and prepare to give the intruder a hot reception?

Andy saw that he must have said something to the larger man, for the other quickly looked toward Zeb. Neither did he show any sign of sudden and overwhelming alarm. Indeed, he even smiled broadly, and looked *pleased*, which about completed Andy's confusion. The mystery was really too deep for him, though when he heard Rob chuckling close by, he began to fancy that the scout master was able to read between the lines better than he had been.

It grew even more mysterious when Andy saw Zeb, their friend Zeb, actually hold out his hand and take the extended digits of the solemn-looking dark-faced man, whose straight figure and black hair made the boy suspect that he might well have some Indian blood in his veins.

Now Zeb was facing the large man, who still sat there and listened to what the Maine woodsman might be saying. When he, too, finally reached up his hand and Zeb eagerly pounced upon it, all at once the wonderful truth broke in upon the bewildered Andy just as a flash of lightning might dart from the clouds to the earth during a storm.

Why, these were not desperate conspirators they had discovered, at all. Their work had been for nothing, save that it was good practice for scouts to be given a chance to show what they could do in the way of creeping up on a suspected enemy's camp. That man with the bronzed skin was Sebattis, the Penobscot guide, and the jovial party, to be sure, he could be no other than Tubby's Uncle George!

It was a pretty severe shock to Andy when this burst upon him so suddenly.

"Well, what d'ye think of that, Rob?" he gasped. "After all, we've run across Uncle George and his other guide; and Zeb's in his good graces again. Well, we're certainly in hard luck one way, and in good another. I'm sorry for you, lieutenant, but we've struck the wrong party. We know this gentleman, who is a rich sportsman. If you look sharp you will see a moose head over there, which shows that, after all, Uncle George managed to get the big bull. Good for him!"

The soldier was keenly disappointed to learn that their fine plans had been wasted; but as Rob expected, he was made of the right kind of stuff and could take things as they came, the bitter with the sweet.

"We're certainly stumped, boys," was what the officer remarked, with a short laugh, such as spoke of chagrin, "if, as you say, this party is one of your friends; he certainly doesn't look much like a desperado, I must confess. I was trying hard to picture him in such a fiendish raid, but couldn't manage it, any way I figured. But let's step up and meet the gentleman. I imagine we stand no chance whatever now of being able to cut off the flight of those cowardly curs."

The three boys were only too glad to avail themselves of the opportunity. Of course, Rob's and Andy's first thought was of Tubby, and how delighted the fat chum would be to learn they had run across his relative. They would have something of importance to tell Uncle George, too.

By now the big sportsman was on his feet, for he saw strangers advancing toward his camp fire from two different directions; and, being a hospitable soul, Uncle George's first thought was to welcome them to the genial blaze, in true sportsman style.

He looked keenly at the two boys in khaki.

"Hello!" he remarked with a chuckle. "I've got a nephew who's proud to be wearing that khaki cloth, and on his account I'm glad to see you."

"How d'ye do, Uncle George?" Andy coolly remarked, as he shook hands, and it was almost comical to see the gentleman stare at him as he hastened to say:

"Well, you seem to know my name, all right, my boy, which strikes me as rather singular. How do you explain that?"

"Oh, Tubby has talked so much about you that we're all calling you Uncle George, sir, begging your pardon for being so familiar," explained audacious Andy, with one of his widest grins.

"'Tubby'!" exclaimed the gentleman. "Why, you must mean my nephew, Robert Hopkins. I remember that his chums do call him by some such outlandish name. You know him, then, which indicates that I was mistaken when I placed you as Canadian Boy Scouts. I reckon you must live in Hampton, down on Long Island?"

"Just what we do, sir," Rob took occasion to remark. "I'm Rob Blake, and this is Andy Bowles, both members of the same Eagle Patrol that Tubby belongs to. You will be still more surprised, I take it, sir, when you learn that your nephew is not over a mile or so away from this spot right now."

"You amaze me, my boy. Whatever brought him away up here in the wilderness? Please explain the mystery, Rob."

"I can do that in a few sentences, Mr. Hopkins," said the scout leader; and with that he told about the paper that it was so necessary for Uncle George to sign before a certain date; and how school being dismissed for two weeks, Tubby and his chums had been dispatched up into Maine to find the sportsman.

This satisfied the gentleman, but there were other mysteries waiting to be explained. He wondered how the boys had met the Canadian soldiers, and why they should all be creeping up on his little camp in such a stealthy fashion.

So Rob thought it just as well to tell him about the amazing things that had happened. Swiftly Rob brought the story down to where the patriotic chums, together with Zeb and Donald, had succeeded in severing the necessary wire, and thus prevented the awful plot from being carried out.

All of this must have been highly entertaining to Uncle George, to judge from the smile on his face, and the many chuckles in which he indulged from time to time. When Rob finished the account the sportsman shook hands all around again and then freed his mind.

"It was excellently carried out, boys, most wonderfully executed, in fact, and I'm certain this gentleman feels under heavy obligations to you all. Donald never would have managed to get over in time to give warning, only for you. Consequently the saving of the bridge, and the munition train as well, lies at your door. I'm also proud of the fact that you are loyal Americans, and that you considered it your bounden duty to stand up for patriotism as you did. Robert will be dearer to me than ever after this, for he seems to be a boy after my own heart."

Then he turned to the lieutenant again, and went on to say in his cordial way:

"I hope this will only be another cause for cementing the friendship of the two great English-speaking races. We have thousands of our boys Over There in the French war trenches, and in the aviation corps, as well as with the Red Cross, doing their bit for humanity and the great cause of a peace that will bless the whole civilized world for ages, and I honestly believe that before long our country will be your ally in this struggle. Now, sir, before you think of starting back to your duty allow me to offer you a cup of hot coffee, and anything in the way of refreshment my larder affords."

The officer was anxious to return with as little delay as possible, for he felt that he had a weighty responsibility resting on his shoulders; but it was hard to resist that smile and those winning ways; so he agreed to linger for, say, half an hour longer. Rob said he, Andy and Donald also would return with him when he went, for they wished to rejoin their chum.

Andy was soon seen examining the monster moose head with its broad horns, and on observing his action the gentleman sportsman called out:

"I've been after that fellow for several seasons now, my boy, and this year we looked for him over at the Tucker Pond; but he led us quite a chase, and we only potted him here this afternoon, while swinging around on the way back to the logging camp."

"Well," remarked Andy, laughing, "we weren't even looking for him, but he paid us a visit, all the same, we've got reason to believe," and then he related how their brush shanty had been partly demolished by the rush of a giant moose, which account amused Uncle George greatly.

CHAPTER XXVI
EVERYBODY SATISFIED

Taken in all, they spent quite a pleasant half hour with Uncle George. Somehow his coffee, brewed there in the camp where his moose trophy lay, seemed to taste like nectar to all concerned.

It turned out, by the way, that the affair was kept quiet as much as possible, for strategic reasons. Perhaps the authorities up in Ottawa believed that to draw a veil of secrecy over the matter would be apt to deter others from attempting similar desperate exploits, where broad publicity might encourage them for the sake of the notoriety it would bring.

Later on the boys, together with the lieutenant and his two men, started for the bridge. Zeb, having been once more reinstated in the good graces of his employer—who had heard all about his return, from Rob in secret—remained in camp, and seemed overjoyed at having his old berth back again. He did not say much to Rob and Andy, being a man of few words, but the way in which he squeezed their hands spoke volumes. Zeb had certainly come to think highly of the scouts in the short time he knew them.

They had no trouble in covering the distance separating them from the railway embankment. They saw nothing of those whom they had hoped to come upon. The fugitives must have managed to get across the line in some fashion.

Tubby was pleased when he heard the signal that told him the other Eagles were close at hand. His astonishment and delight can be easily imagined upon their telling him how they had met his Uncle George and drank coffee at his camp fire. The latter was to stay there in the morning until the boys joined him, when the entire party would start afresh, heading for the logging camp.

The lieutenant made his young guests as comfortable as the limited conditions allowed. He really felt under heavy obligations toward the trio of scouts from across the line, and would never forget them, he promised.

When morning came they concluded to make an early start, for Uncle George had hinted that he would like to have them join him at breakfast. So good-bye's were said, and Donald McGuffey looked quite downcast at parting from the three splendid fellows whom he had come to like exceedingly well during the course of their short acquaintance; for boys get on familiar terms ten times as quickly as men ever do.

Donald had only one burning regret, which was that his years would not permit him enlisting in one of the battalions forming to go across the seas.

"I'm big for my age," were his last words, as he wrung the hand of Andy like a pump handle, "and if this war only keeps up twa mair years, ye ken, I'll more'n likely be allowed to enlist, so as to have a whack at the beasts beyond the seas."

While the scouts may not have felt exactly the same as Donald did, for naturally he was prejudiced by his birth and surroundings, still they gave him credit for valor, as they had seen him put to the test and come through with flying colors. But at the same time they sincerely hoped the terrible carnage would be long over before the Scotch-Canadian boy, who came of a race of fighters, arrived at an age when he might be accepted as a recruit.

They reached the camp of the moose in time to join Uncle George at breakfast, which meal had been postponed a little on account of their expected arrival. Tubby was as happy a chap as any one could well see when he shook hands with his uncle, and was then and there embraced by the veteran sportsman. Tubby actually reddened with confusion, but no one could resist the cheery laugh of Uncle George, and this action on his part told how his chubby nephew had risen in his regard.

As the gentleman was very wealthy, and had no children of his own, sly Andy later on told Tubby he ought to consider himself a very lucky fellow indeed; which insidious remark caused honest Tubby to indignantly say he never had the faintest thought of getting in the good graces of his uncle for any pecuniary benefit that might accrue to him.

After a jolly breakfast they started for the logging camp.

Uncle George kept Tubby and Andy busy relating many interesting things that had happened to the scouts, not only on this momentous occasion but under other conditions.

"It strikes me," was the opinion Uncle George advanced later on, when he had listened with tremendous interest to accounts of their different visits, "that fortune has picked you boys as her especial favorites. You have been given the most wonderful opportunities for *doing things*! Yes, and while you are all so modest about boasting of your achievements I can read between the lines and understand why success so often perches on your banner. It is partly because you deserve it; but in the main I'm inclined to believe the principal factor in your success comes from the fact that in Rob Blake here you have an ideal leader, who knows his business from alpha to omega, the beginning and the end of scoutcraft!"

At that splendid endorsement Rob turned fiery red, and tried to disclaim any greater share of the credit than each one of his chums was fairly entitled to; but both Andy and Tubby vociferously negatived this assertion and assured shrewd Uncle George that he had "hit the nail squarely on the head."

What a glorious week the boys did pass in that lumber camp! The days seemed far too short to encompass all the "stunts" they had planned by the light of the preceding night's jolly fire, where it was their habit to sit around and listen to Uncle George relate some of the peculiar adventures in his long and adventurous life. In turn, they would tell him further incidents connected with their doings as scouts.

How they did hate to say good-bye when it became necessary to break away from that hallowed spot, which would always remain green in their memories since some of the happiest days of their lives were spent there! But that important paper had to be taken back in due time, Uncle George having gone over to the nearest town on the border to sign the same in the presence of a justice and notary. Besides, most cruel thought of all, school would commence the following week, if the epidemic had been gotten under control, and they could not be excused from their classes simply because the hunting was fine up in Maine.

Of course, in such stirring times those wide-awake scouts of Hampton were more than likely to see further happenings come their way; and should any of these be worthy of placing before the reader, be sure that pleasing duty will not long be withheld. Until such time arrives this must suffice.

THE END.